R...

To

The Ridley children

With love from the

The Dean

Keith

WHEN DUSK COMES CREEPING

By the same author

The Seven Deadly Sins

WHEN DUSK COMES CREEPING

Stories of the Sinister

LANYON JONES

WILLIAM KIMBER · LONDON

First published in 1985 by
WILLIAM KIMBER & CO. LIMITED
100 Jermyn Street, London SW1Y 6EE

© Keith Lanyon Jones, 1985

ISBN 0 7183 0561 2

Photoset in North Wales by
Derek Doyle & Associates Mold, Clwyd
and printed in Great Britain by
Biddles Limited, Guildford, Surrey

This book is dedicated
to the pupils of Rugby School
in reciprocation for the
amount of entertainment
they have given me

Contents

Preface   9

I   The Old Boy Network
      I do not like thee, Doctor Fell   11

II   The Ferryman
      Come, let's to bed, says Sleepy-head   33

III   The Secret Garden
      Mary, Mary, quite contrary   51

IV   Déjà Vu
      Little Miss Muffet   73

V   House Spirit
      In a dark, dark wood   91

VI   The Ship in a Bottle
      Bobby Shafto's gone to sea   103

VII   The Call of the Piper
      Tom, he was a Piper's Son   119

VIII All Is Not As It Seems
      Little Red Riding Hood   139

Preface

When dusk comes gently creeping,
And stars begin to peep,
There comes a little Sandman
To lull you off to sleep.

The Sandman in this rhyme sounds such a benign little character when spoken of to sleepy children; they are hurried up the stairs with coaxing that he's coming ...

Yet how many of such lightly spoken rhymes as this have a deeper meaning, a more sinister undertone, a past history. A warning, perhaps, from our traditional teachings of the young, that now we hear as only the faintest of echoes. It is possible that such traditional rhymes, tales and characters, hold some purpose beyond merely the intention to entertain.

The interpretation of 'Ring-a-ring o' roses' is well known: the plague – the mark of the ring of roses the first sign. The 'pocket full of posies' is the nosegay held to ward off the infection. Sneezing is the second stage – and 'all fall down' is obvious.

Wee Willie Winkie is another rhyme which, after close inspection, may not be found so cosy as at first imagined. Who is this emaciated little figure scurrying through the dark? Is it really a nightgown that he wears, or is it some other white garment fitted for a longer sleep? And one is left to puzzle the questions:

Why does he tap on the windows?
Why cry through the locks?
What is it that he wants with the children?

They are the rhymes and stories we remember from childhood, and in childhood too we experience the pleasurable dread of at one and the same time feeling safe and warm, yet pondering what may lie in the shadows beyond the firelight; beyond the comforting glow or beyond the tight drawn darkened curtains. An unknown world of cold phantoms and unspoken horrors outside our parents' influence.

In adulthood the fears recede – only in occasional and unfamiliar old buildings, where there might be passageways and winding staircases leading ... one knows not where. Old books on long undusted shelves that when opened are discovered to be filled with strange writings and unknown symbols. Or, coming across a shuttered door one is arrested by a scuffling or a whimpering in the dark. And the old terrors struggle to the surface, to war against our sense of order ... and with an effort they are extinguished again by the prejudices of adulthood.

In such ways these stories came to be written, around the themes of Nursery Rhymes, old tales and ancient buildings.

But before you read on, a short explanation: The themes of 'The Old Boy Network' and 'House Spirit' may be felt to be too similar. I hope the similarity of setting doesn't detract too much from the enjoyment. One was invented to entertain a couple of very bored pupils in the school sanatorium, and the other I wrote for the school magazine – they therefore both reflect something of the 'Public School' ethos.

A number of people thought that Canon Cedric and his friend Geoffrey, the Verger, were too cowardly when they appeared in the story 'Covetousness' in my earlier collection entitled *The Seven Deadly Sins*. I think they would probably have felt ashamed of themselves, so I've given them a chance to redeem their good name in the story 'All is not as it seems'.

I hope these tales go part way to restoring the nursery rhyme to its rightful place as the lair of the sinister rather than a mere homely entertainment for children.

I hope you enjoy them.

K.L.J.

I

The Old Boy Network

I do not like thee, Dr Fell …

'It's a marvellous opportunity. I don't know what your objection could possibly be.' Richard Sampson folded his newspaper vigorously to emphasise his annoyance; he stared at his wife across the breakfast table.

She looked back at him with unusually cold eyes, her mouth a straight line. She looked even more handsome when she was annoyed, her eyes flashing, the lustre of her red hair catching the light as she shook her head.

'You don't know what the school's like. How can you contemplate sending our daughter to a place you've never even visited?'

Her husband lighted upon the error.

'But Victoria's not our daughter, is she? She is your daughter, and Roger went to Bloefield – that's the point, that's the point. No daughter of mine would ever be allowed in, nor a son for that matter.'

'It didn't do Roger any good though, did it – as well you know.'

Richard felt he could sympathise a little with her objections. It was based on her loathing for her first husband. It had been a blessing for everyone that he'd been killed. But that wasn't the point, and now Victoria had the chance of going there. Even though he hadn't had a public school education himself, Richard would make sure his step-daughter had the benefit.

'All the men I know of who went there have done incredibly well. It's got a remarkable record –'

'In lots of ways,' she interrupted, beginning to look sullen as his arguments in favour of the proposal mounted.

'It's sick, like some kind of secret society, codes and signs and all that …' she searched for the word '… nonsense.'

But that word didn't fit either. She meant something more sinister than that, something somehow malevolent.

He took advantage of her silence.

'If you've got a good thing going, why bother to share it? I can see the reason for the exclusivism. But if all the old boys are doing so well that they can restrict entry just to their sons, then that must be a good advert.'

'So why are they suddenly offering places for daughters?'

'I don't know.'

She really was being astonishingly aggravating about the whole thing – quite unlike her usual self.

'Most other public schools have had girls in the sixth form for ages – it's just falling in line with the rest. Anyway, it's more healthy.'

His wife gave a dry laugh. It sounded a little hysterical.

'That's the first time I've heard anything from Bloefield described as healthy. You've never been there, you don't know what it's like. The atmosphere gives me the creeps.'

'That's only the effect of a male environment. All boys' boarding schools are a bit odd." He spoke from no knowledge. 'But its record is second to none; it's a great opportunity and I'm going to send her. It will do her A-levels a power of good.'

She glared at him – mute. It was his money. He had provided her with everything, even given her and Victoria sanctuary when Roger was still alive and becoming more violent. This was the first time they had really disagreed about anything; she would have to give in.

He felt able to placate her a little.

'I really think we ought to go there and see for ourselves.' But she sounded suddenly tired – resigned.

'I've been haunted by that terrible place for too long – you go on your own. You see. You make the decision.'

She turned to her newspaper, burying her feelings, giving in.

Of course he felt sorry for her. She had had a bad deal with an almost insane man, but she could hardly blame Roger's behaviour on his old school. It was true he didn't know much about the place. He hadn't realised until now that all the staff were old boys as well. That certainly seemed a little unusual, but he had seen the products of the place, and that surely must be the judge. Some of the most successful men in the city were Old Bloefieldians. The Army too seemed to sport a good number of them in its higher echelons. And he remembered the comment someone had made: 'Of course, they do kill well', but that was only sour grapes of course. In all walks of life, power, influence, they stuck tgoether, helping one another. The only area Bloefield never seemed to score was the Church. To his knowledge it had never produced a Bishop – that was funny really. The founder had been an eminent churchman of sorts. He frowned. Well, perhaps not eminent; he remembered something from university days about Dr Fell, but he didn't remember its being very complimentary – just 'well-known'. It teased his mind like an irritating crossword clue. How could a Victorian churchman be 'well-known' without being eminent?

'What was it that Dr Fell was famous for?'

He immediately wished he hadn't spoken. She put her paper down, her face looked drawn, a look he hadn't seen since before Roger's death.

'I don't like Dr Fell.'

It was a ridiculous thing for her to say, putting the man in the present tense. He must have been dead for a hundred years at least.

'Oh it doesn't matter.' He feigned not noticing, passing it off. Yet she stared at him. It made him feel uncomfortable, and he coughed, leaning back and rustling his paper, groping for his coffee cup.

Now what was it about Dr Fell? It still teased his mind. He would have to look him up.

He made the journey, as she had suggested, without his wife. Victoria had been invited for interview. It unnerved him a little; he thought she wouldn't need to be interviewed – his awareness of the old boy net was not as perfect as it could have been.

As soon as they came within sight of the great grey wall that marked the boundary of the park, his step-daughter seemed to sit up and take more notice. The wall seemed to march on for miles as they drove along the road outside, and she grew ever more animated as they passed each barred gate. The next, surely the next, would be the open gate to the main drive.

And as they had driven thus his feelings had somehow changed. It was probably Margaret's silent disapproval that had caused it. But as he drove along the outside of the great high wall and passed, one by one, the black and barred gates of the subsidiary drives he saw for a fleeting moment, not a park at all, but the dark crowded trees of a great unkempt wood. A feeling of disquiet arose, an uncertainty about his wisdom, a doubt about the place. The sight of those narrow driveways beyond the bars, leading away into the tangled wood, away from the light of the high road, into a dark interior – somehow it depressed him; it was another world.

When the park gates finally appeared, his apprehension was assuaged by the grandeur of the entrance. To belong to such a school – what could that do for his adopted child?

The baroque pillars of the entrance were surmounted by heavy effigies of double-headed rams. An enormous coat of arms stood over the high wrought-iron gates; it bore the same insignia – the double-headed ram. They drove in, past the flanking gatehouses, and as he passed by, he saw the kennels with the baying Doberman dogs – protection for the precious inmates, he surmised.

The drive swept down and up again, a broad expanse of gravel. The dark woods that marched alongside gave way eventually to open parkland, and then, after the lake with its curious temple-like building and a curve of the drive there on the crest of a hill above them, the school itself. A great heavy baroque pile, a mass of chimneys and domes against the sky, with what he assumed to be the chapel to one side, an extraordinary building with classical pillars and a vast green canopy of tarnished copper. As they passed he noticed it, too, possessed the double-headed ram insignia over the lintel.

He had been welcomed cordially enough but he didn't like feeling the odd-man-out. Most of the other fathers seemed to know one another – and they gave each other that curious handshake. He had already shaken hands with a number of them and each had reacted in the same way. A passing look of puzzlement and then a polite smile – distanced. He felt like an outsider at a Masons' lodge meeting.

But Victoria was in her element – quite an extraordinary transformation. She had always been beautiful like her mother, with her complexion and massed red hair, but of late she had been sullen and withdrawn, a very private girl. But here she seemed to blossom, to come into her element. Although he felt out of place, she seemed immediately accepted. The Chaplain and Headmaster particularly seemed to take to her, and she chatted to them with an ease that left him rather envious.

He didn't know whether it was the proud parent in him or not, but all eyes seemed to be on her when she walked into a room. She certainly seemed to make an impression. He admitted to himself that she looked quite stunning in her white spring dress and her red hair falling around her shoulders.

The day seemed to go well – and all the masters they met seemed pleased to see her. Only one thing irritated him about the visit: as he hadn't been there before he had been offered a guided tour of the buildings. A very polite senior boy showed him around, Victoria going off with a group of prospective entrants. He had known the chapel service had been timed for five o'clock, but his guide thought it six, so when they met up again, Victoria said he had missed it. It was such a shame, she said; it was the most interesting service she had ever been to, not like 'church' at all. He asked if he could see inside the chapel, it was such an interesting looking building, but was told that it was locked after service, so alas he couldn't.

The day ended there, and they began their journey home. Victoria was full of the school at the beginning of the journey. She seemed to like the Chaplain, but when asked couldn't recall what it was in the service that she had particularly liked. In fact she didn't seem to be able to remember anything about it at all apart from there being no crosses in the building. She said that there had been this big throne-like chair in the centre, with rams' heads for arms, and feet like cloven hoofs, but that was all she could remember.

He thought that interesting and expected that the lack of Christian ornament was probably 'Low Church'. He had heard somewhere that most public schools were like that.

After a while they settled into silence. It was a long journey and Victoria slept on the way back. He occasionally looked at her, so motionless did she lie; a kind of exhausted non-dreaming sleep that one associates with hospital patients after an operation. But she was all right and he surmised it was the exhaustion after giving so much of herself in one eventful day.

As he drove he puzzled over his ambivalent reaction. He had to be honest, he didn't feel at home in the environment, but that probably was because he was unaccustomed to it. It was incredibly cut off behind that high wall, and those woods ... He hadn't much taken to the cliqueyness of the other fathers there, or that strangely polite and insistent boy who had kept him away from the chapel service. But that was probably his own defensiveness about his not being a public school boy himself. It was a marvellous opportunity, for academic success if for nothing more. One positive thing did feel odd though: the strange way they spoke of Dr Fell, the founder. He supposed that that was what is described as 'inculcation of a sense of history', but he didn't feel they had to speak about him in such hushed tones, and always in the present tense, as if he were still running the place. Perhaps he would never understand places like that – it would probably be best to let Victoria decide, he thought. On balance, he decided he wouldn't pressurise her to go.

But go she did. After the letter from the Headmaster, it would seem churlish in the extreme not to send her. 'Only a very few of the girl candidates were deemed suitable and I have much pleasure in offering Victoria a place for early September.'

They didn't realise how few until she actually got there. Of the other three girls who had received offers of entry, one had apparently become ill with some unspecified ailment, or so the Chaplain said, and the other two had had terrible accidents. It was horribly unfortunate and a great shame for Victoria of course, but as it had all happened at the last minute, they all hoped that Victoria wouldn't mind being the first female 'guinea pig', as it were.

Her father assured them that of course it would be all right, although he didn't feel quite as confident. He was assured that Victoria would have the best of treatment and accommodation, actually in the Headmaster's house. No harm could possibly come to her there – and anyway, they hoped that there might be the other girl by January, if she recovered from her illness. Alas, the other two girls were so terribly ill after their separate accidents that they would never finish their schooling.

On enquiry, he was told that one had been out riding and her horse had bolted in front of a train. It had been killed outright, but incredibly her life had been saved. The other had been at her parents' home on her own and somehow the house had caught fire. She would be needing plastic surgery on her face and arms for at least eighteen months.

Sampson was dismayed at the awfulness of the happenings, and readily agreed to the Chaplain's suggestion that they shouldn't tell Victoria the details lest it upset her at the start of her new school life.

The school did not permit parents to visit during term-time, which seemed to Sampson a sensible precaution against disruption of the academic process, and, contrary to his wife's worries, the first few letters were full of praise for the staff's teaching, the courteous behaviour of the boys and the kindness of the Headmaster and the Chaplain to her. She felt, she said, like a princess – everything she could have wanted was provided for her. Not a thing was too much bother in making her happy and content, and her room in the Headmaster's house was 'quite divine'. She described it in detail: almost circular, it occupied a tower room and was furnished almost entirely in white. The only thing she didn't like were the portraits that hung round the walls. She said she felt they were looking at her, a collection of portraits of young boys. Curiously they all had red hair like her own; she thought they must be the children of the family who had once lived in the house.

So the first letters were ecstatic, but by the first week in October a different note had introduced itself:

Dearest Mummy and Richard,
    As you probably know all our letters are read before we send them ...

This raised an eyebrow, but Sampson knew the practice of censorship was something a lot of institutions had as a rule and so he explained it away. The next letter, written on the twelfth of the month, included a rather odd passage: 'I do not like Dr Fell, but the reason for this I cannot say ...'

At this Sampson was a little perturbed and phoned the school, asking to speak with Victoria. He received a polite response from the Headmaster's housekeeper, but she was certainly not enthusiastic to let him speak to his daughter, but he insisted and Victoria was brought to the phone.

The pleasantries were short lived.

'Hello, darling.'

'Hello, Richard ...' She sounded a little distracted.

'Are you all right – your letter sounded a little odd?'

'Yes ... Just a minute ...' A pause while she apparently shut a door.

'Hello, Richard. I don't think I've got much time ... you know that trick with invisible ink you showed me, well in my next letter ...' There was a faint click, as if another receiver had been picked up. Victoria was silent for a moment, and then she spoke again, a different tone in her voice – bright and cheerful.

'Well thank you for telling me, Richard. I'm sure dear old Felix will get over it. He's such a silly old dog, isn't he?'

She paused, but he was too stupefied to respond. She continued:

'I'm certain there's no need for me to come home to see him. I'm absolutely fine. The school's marvellous and the Headmaster couldn't be kinder. Give Felix a pat for me, won't you? But you'd better not ring again. I think it's probably a bit of an imposition on the Headmaster. Look carefully at my next letter – I'll tell you how I am. Thanks for phoning. I really must go now. Bye.'

'Bye, darling.' The phone went dead.

Sampson sat in the chair looking at the receiver, the disengaged sound purring quietly.

He wondered whether to tell Margaret, but that would bring about enormous repercussions and, however extraordinary the conversation, she had said she was all right, she hadn't wanted to rush back home. There was nothing too terribly wrong then, there couldn't be anything sinister in it, otherwise she would have said. Maybe it was a kind of lark – like midnight feasts. He had read of such things in boarding schools. Invisible ink sounded clandestine enough for that. He decided to wait and see. He again picked up the most recent letter which bore the double-headed ram insignia and the telephone number: 'I do not like Dr Fell, but the reason for this I cannot say.'

He would make inquiries about Dr Fell in the morning – and then await the next letter. It was a candle you needed to warm the paper, and then you could read the writing between the lines; he remembered telling her that.

*

He had been a member of the Halldon Library for years but had never really used it much before. But it was just the place to gather the information he needed now, and the librarian was very helpful, with an encyclopaedic knowledge.

'There are several books that mention him, sir. But he was a secretive kind of man, and you have to know where to look.'

The slight, bespectacled figure led him up a flight of steps past rows upon rows of leatherbound volumes. Along a balcony overlooking yet more booklined shelves, up another flight and then yet another.

'If you can sit here, sir, I won't be a minute. One mustn't get Dr Fell muddled with the other one – the seventeenth-century Dr Fell.'

Sampson sat at a desk looking out over the void above the rest of the library. Other inquirers and men of letters moved about quietly far below. In any usual building a babble of sound would rise up, but here the gentle easing of a chair or the slow turning of large pages was all that disturbed the silence.

After some few minutes the librarian re-appeared with two slim volumes.

'As luck would have it,' he spoke softly, 'there's another gentleman just about to borrow the major work, *Dr Fell and his Disciples*; that's the one you really want, sir. A very rare copy by Fr Jerome Macleod, very critical too it is.' He looked down at the two volumes he held.

'Not much in these, I'm afraid – of course in a way he was like Arnold at Rugby, not as great of course, and nowhere near as influential.'

He looked down at Sampson, his steel-rimmed spectacles glinting in the shafts of light. Sampson looked up at the man.

'Do you know anything about him?'

'Oh, sir …' The librarian paused, letting out his breath slowly.

'Let me see.' He scratched his scant hair, grimacing slightly.

'He was a contemporary with Thomas Arnold, I suppose – a Doctor of Divinity – but then almost everyone was.'

'He produced some very curious ideas.'

The librarian paused. 'Yes, that's right. He had a chair in theology at Cambridge, but he lost it. There was a terrible to-do about it, some works he produced about necromancy if I remember aright.' The librarian paused again, mistaking the look in his face. 'You know, sir, communication with the dead – predicting the future.'

'Yes – yes, I knew that.'

'Oh, sorry, for a moment I thought you hadn't followed.'

'No, no, I was just thinking of something else, that's all.'

Sampson put his hand in his jacket pocket. Yes, it was still there, Victoria's latest letter.

'I think he based it on Saul's calling up of Samuel – you know, the Witch of Endor.'

'Yes, I know the passage.'

'Well, as far as I can recall, he had to leave Cambridge – and took a group of quite brilliant young graduates with him. They set up a school together, Bloefield I think it's called. Quite different from Arnold's philosophy, of course. You could almost call him the antithesis of Arnold, and all that Arnold stood for.' He paused again.

'Of course, Arnold was a Christian.' He spoke almost to himself.

'Whatever do you mean?' The outburst was too loud; Sampson had forgotten to keep his voice down and several heads turned to look up from below to enquire – the most genteel form of disapproval. They went back to their books. He felt like saying 'Sorry', but merely turned to repeat the question in a hissed whisper.

'Whatever do you mean? Dr Fell was a clergyman, wasn't he?'

'Well, almost every intelligent scholar was in those days – but don't take my word for it, sir – it's all in Macleod's book – about the accusation of ...' he paused, lowering his voice even further ... 'Devil worship ... Ah, here's that gentleman now. Perhaps you could arrange to borrow the book after him.'

A youngish man with sandy hair came along the balcony. Sampson thought he recognised him. He, too, had a look of recognition in his eyes. He extended a hand to Sampson, who got up, taking the proffered hand – a strange handshake. The younger man looked slightly puzzled.

'Sorry. I thought I knew you.' He withdrew his hand.

'Mr Sampson is the gentleman who wanted to borrow the book after you, sir. If you would leave your name at the desk?'

The librarian said the words before Sampson could stop him.

Sampson wished he hadn't said his name. The younger

man's eyes had widened slightly, but the polite smile didn't waver.

'Yes, certainly. I'll leave it at the desk; I won't be needing the book for long, Mr Sampson.' The younger man paused, seemed to take thought for a moment and then patted his breast pocket. He turned to the librarian.

'I don't suppose I could borrow your pen to write it with, could I? I don't seem to have mine with me.' The librarian happily responded, handing him his fountain pen.

'If you could leave it on the desk, sir, it's rather precious, I've had it for a long time.' The man looked at the pen and seemed to say 'So much the better' – but Sampson could not be sure. He put the pen in his inside jacket pocket. The young man gave his polite smile again.

'Thank you so much. I do hate using biros, and that's all they have on the desk.' He nodded and was gone, along the gallery and down the steps.

Sampson left the library soon afterwards. The librarian was disconcerted by there being no name and address left and, more to the point, the stranger had taken his pen. But he thought the young man would return soon.

'If you could call again sir – early next week?'

＊

The letter arrived on Tuesday morning of the following week. Sampson scanned the banal comments, wishing to get away in private to warm it over a candle and read Victoria's more candid comments. But Margaret sat on at the breakfast table reading her newspaper.

'Oh dear – what an awful thing.' Sampson looked up from the letter.

'What's that, my dear?'

'You're a member of the Halldon Library, aren't you?'

'Yes, why?'

'There's been the most tragic accident – the librarian's been killed.'

Sampson sat still. The picture of the bespectacled man hovered before him.

'He was on the top balcony checking some books – he was up a step ladder or something, and fell over the edge. Look, do you see?'

She handed him the paper, but he could barely read it.

A photograph of the front of the building and a description of what had happened. The library had just closed. There were only two people in the building. The assistants heard the cry and the crash as he hit the bookcases below. It was obviously an accident – there hadn't been anyone near him. There was a short description of the librarian, a reference to the obituary. The library would remain shut for at least a week.

It was a coincidence of course – an accident. No one had been near him when it happened. The young man's polite smile hovered before him, and he re-heard the librarian's voice – almost as if he were in the room.

'Mr Sampson is the gentleman –' Sampson had a tingling sensation on the hairs of his neck.

He took the letter and left the room, going into the study. He already had a candle and matches waiting. He lit the candle and held the paper near the flame. The brown words began to appear before him between the neat ink handwriting:

> Some very funny things go on here. This is the only way I can tell you about it ... We aren't having a Christmas carol service – apparently they never do ... But

Well at least that didn't sound desperate. He felt relief from the rising panic of the last few moments He read on as the words became plain.

> But there's a lot of singing at night – strange songs – from the chapel – like chanting. We have a lot of services in the evening, but the Chaplain doesn't do them. I like him, but the Headmaster gives me the creeps. He takes most of the services dressed in funny robes. There's a glass globe in the centre that turns round with sort of sparkling light in it.

Everyone looks at it. I don't, though – it makes me feel too
odd, sort of dizzy and sick. There's a funny thing about the
school, lots of the boys have died here over the years. I
reckon it's about one every five years since the school was
started by Dr Fell. We have their names read out – like a role
of honour. They are all buried in the chapel – not one of
their families wanted them buried at home. Funny, isn't it?

Must close. No more space. I'm all right really, just odd.
See you at the end of term.
                                          Luv V.

It was part relief, part a feeling of rising apprehension. He
tried to analyse the facts. Only the facts. He mustn't jump to
conclusions. It was, as Victoria said, just odd – very odd – but
that's all it could be. He didn't know much about schools like
that – they were a thing apart, they were probably all odd in
their way. He had heard of rituals before, seen films about it –
but that was with the boys, not the masters. He didn't know
what to think, apart from the fact that she would come home in
two weeks' time for Christmas. They would certainly sort it all
out then. Just two weeks away, Saturday 22nd December.

The following week he worried. Was he right? Was he being
foolish? He certainly couldn't speak to Margaret. He consoled
himself with the nearness of the Christmas holiday and awaited
the next letter.

He should really read the volumes the librarian had given
him, but they seemed entirely about other people and had no
indexes so he couldn't find any information about Dr Fell until
he read through the whole lot.

On Tuesday the 18th, the next letter arrived. As soon as he
saw it, he realised something must have happened. It was
particularly long and full of long drawn-out inanities to cover
the space of her real message. He got to the study as quickly as
possible, locking the door behind him.

Things are very strange here – and becoming more peculiar.
Three things have happened. I was awoken late in the night

(on Friday) by whispering outside my door. It sounded like a whole lot of people, adult voices and young ones, too, I could see lights and moving shadows under the door, as if they were holding a candelit procession along the corridor and there was a great deal of chanting – it wasn't English, or Latin, it was more guttural – I think it could have been Hebrew – I'm not sure. It was almost as if they had started outside my room. I think I was woken up by them assembling. When they'd gone, I followed them. They went to the chapel. The door was left ajar so I could see something of what was going on. I saw the Headmaster there in his funny robes. They all gathered round the ram's head throne – bowing down and chanting. Each of the boys had to pass by. The Headmaster had a bowl on a large table in front of the throne and he dipped a long knife into the bowl and touched them on the forehead. But the funny thing was that there wasn't anything in the bowl – it was as if they were rehearsing some kind of ritual. But we aren't having a carol service; I can't understand it. I slipped away not long after that in case I was found out, but the chanting went on and on and got quite loud later. I've heard the chanting before – late at night – they've probably been rehearsing for a couple of weeks now. The atmosphere's getting very tense – there's a kind of excitement in the air. I can't really describe it but it's very odd and they don't talk about it to me. Another thing that's odd is that I've had my hair-brush stolen, and then it was returned again but all the hair that was in it had gone. I had meant to clean it out but hadn't bothered – it's very strange. Who would want some of my hair?

But the really weird thing is what I found in the room above mine in the Headmaster's house. I'd heard a lot of noise up there on occasions, a lot of shuffling about. When there was no one about I went up to see what was in the room. It was lined with shelves with dolls on them – sort of clay dolls – and they were all broken with arms off or heads separated from the bodies. Each shelf was labelled with the date of a year and funny sorts of symbols.

But weirdest of all was the pattern in the centre of the floor – marked out in chalk – sort of circles and triangles, and in the middle were four dolls – like the others, all damaged. One of them had its face all burned off, and the hair was singed. Three of them had what looked like real hair. They were the female dolls. One had been smashed under a model train. The train wheels were embedded right into it. Another has pins stuck into it – most around the neck. The fourth was a male doll by its clothing, it was hanging over a bookcase as if it had been thrown against it – all its head was broken in. Isn't that the weirdest thing?

Sampson re-read the passage: 'What would anyone want with some of my hair?' Where else recently had he heard of someone taking something of someone else's? He couldn't recall. The candle flame began to scorch the paper of the letter and he forgot the thought as he stopped it burning and got on with reading the rest of the secret message.

I think the Headmaster must be really kinked to have things like that in his house. I think I might go and talk to the Chaplain about it – he seems the only sane one in the school. I'm not sure I want to stay here. They keep talking about Dr Fell – it's almost as if he's still alive. Must close. See you soon.

Love Victoria

Sampson put the letter down and breathed out a long, deep sigh. He would go to collect her immediately. He looked at the date on his watch. He would be collecting her next Saturday anyway – would it be worth all the fuss to drive in and take her away without excuse? Of course it could all be coincidence – each item a coincidence. It was the most extraordinary series of incidents. But what could they all be up to – if it were true? They were obviously a bunch of lunatics and she certainly wouldn't go back there. But was there anything else to it – at the latter end of the twentieth century? It seemed utterly incredible to a sane man. What could they possibly be up to?

*

On the Thursday night of that week Victoria was again disturbed in the dead of night, roused by the hushed whispers beyond her door. She determined to investigate fully. Already dressed in jeans, she pulled on a dark jumper. As the flickering candlelight moved away from outside her room she slipped out of the door to follow them. Again they processed into the chapel and gathered around the throne. She managed to slip into the back stalls without being noticed, they were engrossed in practising their ritual.

Again the gathering around the throne and the long table. She noticed that it too bore the insignia, at each corner the ram's head, its horns splayed out to form the edge of the table top; the feet of the table cloven hoofs.

The Headmaster stood before the table in his long robes, and in front of him the bowl, the shining curved knife, and something else. It was another clay doll, but this one was larger than the others she had seen and – she strained her eyes in the flickering candlelight – it had red hair.

She controlled her rising panic as she watched. The rhythmic chanting stopped. The central figure raised his hands and spoke, his voice high-pitched and quavering:

'Tonight, O Master. The Eve of the Great Return – we thy humble servants ...'

The hooded figures repeated the words:

'We thy humble servants.'

'Gather in welcome, O Master.'

'We come, O Master.'

There was a smell, a smell like incense – sweet but too sweet. A smell like new mown grass, its sweetness on the verge of the sickly, on the edge of being the revolting, a smell of corrupt vegetation. She saw something like mist drifting along the floor. The music started again and the chanting mesmeric, irresistible.

'Come, O Master, come to receive the gift we offer – the red and the white of the purity of the offering ...'

'The Eve of the Return,' they responded.

The strange smelling mist drifted up and around the figure in his robes, and the flickering light bemused her eyesight. She wasn't really sure at first but the mist was being drawn from the floor and the walls creeping in a steady movement around him.

She flinched and took her hands away from the wood carved stall as that too gave up its wreaths of curling greyness. She looked around: the chanting was louder, the curling mist emanated now from all the walls and pillars of the building, as well as the floor. She saw it moving in from outside, around the edge of the door left ajar.

It seemed to emanate from the whole fabric of the place, as the chanting rose and fell it gathered in banking waves, not around the central figure as she had first thought, but beyond him. It gathered at the throne, a mounting whirl of grey mist converging and condensing as the lights flickered and the chanting rose and fell.

'The Eve of the awakening, O Master – we implore your return ... implore your return.'

'O spirit of the School, come forth!' A cacophony, a chorus of deep groans from the gathered assembly, and then she saw it, not so much coming out of the mist but rather a growing from it.

She felt her eyes widen; she was not afraid of what she saw but transfixed – enthralled – drawn into the experience of those others gathered around. The figure on the throne.

It raised itself, as if still half asleep, one arm extended up to stretch great powerful muscles unused for a long time. One of the heads, the head of a goat leaning back, its curved horns pointing down its back, its wide mouth open – a silent baying. The other arm extended, a long fingered hand passed over its other face – the face of the man. As he looked around, his goat-like eyes blazing red and a smile of welcome on his lips.

*

'Ah Mr Sampson ...' The Headmaster's voice sounded pleasant down the phone, normal. Sampson looked out of his office window. London – sensible, material London in the clear cold sunlight. What would his friends think of him, arranging a complicated lie to a school master to allay his own ridiculous fears.

'Yes, I received your letter this morning. Of course we will expect you tomorrow. Term ends at 11 a.m. you can certainly take Victoria away then.'

'Yes, I'm glad you wrote to explain about her grandmother's illness. I quite understand if she doesn't come back immediately after the break.'

Sampson felt all this to be further proof of his own stupidity. The Headmaster was perfectly sane, and obviously a reasonable man. He regretted the letter, full of the most outrageous nonsense – 'Grandmother dying – have to be there ...' He had hand-written it in his haste – and not wanting his secretary to see what he was saying but he hadn't wanted to face the man on Saturday, just to pick her up and get out. By the following morning he felt moved to phone to try to cement the frail tissues of lies with some kind of personal assurance. The conversation only enhanced his feelings of stupidity. Probably Victoria was perpetrating some complicated joke and the whole thing was a nonsense. He only half listened to the final words from the Headmaster.

'Yes ... I'm very glad to have something of yours in my hands, Mr Sampson – the letter is just fine.'

He paused, seeming to feel he had to explain himself. He added.

'We need written confirmation of these things, of course.'

Sampson muttered his goodbyes and apologies and was just about to put the receiver down when the Headmaster asked.

'One further question, Mr Sampson ...?

'You will be driving your Volvo, I presume?'

It was an odd question – Sampson assured him that he would.

'It's just that we want to recognise you of course ... to make it all as quick as possible ... your collecting Victoria, that is.'

*

She sat in a high-backed armchair opposite the Chaplain. His rooms overlooked the lake, and it shone beautifully in the westering sunlight. It was almost dusk.

He had an understanding face. He sat with his back to the window, bowed down slightly, his hands held before him, he nodded as she proceeded with her story.

She wanted to get it all right. She had to tell someone and he was the only one she trusted. Last night's experiences had been incredible. She spent the rest of the night awake, working over what she had witnessed, going back over details she had picked up – constructing her evidence into an intelligible pattern. She wouldn't return she was certain of that. As soon as her father arrived in the morning she would leave the place for good.

He smiled as she finished.

'Yes, I see ... You've marshalled some fascinating ideas ...'

He sat for a few moments looking at her.

'Let's get it right – this – "thing" you saw. It was part man and part ... goat?' He raised an enquiring eyebrow – not in derision, but as an actual question.

She nodded.

'And you reckon it's what's left of Dr Fell – a transmuted Dr Fell.'

She nodded again, picking at her finger nails. It all sounded terribly far-fetched, hearing it from someone else in daylight.

'And he was "called back" by the Headmaster?' He waved a hand in the air to explain his meaning.

'Called up – rather – from the fabric of the place.'

She affirmed it with a nod.

'Yes.' He sat back eyeing her, but not unkindly, more reflectively. She was after all talking about his colleagues – people he'd known for a long time, people who'd kept this secret to themselves. He would obviously have a right to be sceptical – questioning. But he was being very fair with this information. He wasn't dismissing her as stupid. She waited for what he had to say.

'You reckon that Dr Fell is still here – and that there is some kind of secret cult – based on the school – with rituals ... about death, and coming back – necromancy. Do you know what that means?'

She didn't.

'It's about using the dead as a way of finding out the future – of being able to predict what's going to happen.'

He smiled at her.

'It would be jolly useful in business, wouldn't it – knowing what was going to happen? You would do pretty well for yourself – if it were possible. The people involved could become very influential.'

She supposed they would – she hadn't thought about that.

'And the deaths at the school, you reckon they are some kind of ritual killing?' He raised an eyebrow. 'To give Dr Fell something to return for? A kind of sacrifice offered for information perhaps?'

She hadn't gone that far – but what he was saying made sense. She had been right to talk to him. He followed her train of thought, but with more knowledge somehow …

'The red and the white you mentioned. There's always been something special about people with red hair – in Satan Worship, an acceptable sacrifice. The portraits in your room for example.'

Yes, of course – she had been a fool. The names so often repeated in chapel, like a roll of honour – they could be all those boys.

And if their fathers were involved, had got some benefit out of it, were part of the cult from their childhood up, initiated whilst at school – they wouldn't want the bodies at home. It would be a privilege to give them to Dr Fell – or whatever he had become – a kind of thank offering, a sustenance for the cult to continue. That's why the School only admitted sons of former pupils – it was to keep everything in the cult. She began to see it all.

'Of course, as you say the cult would have to defend itself – certain things would be expedient. The clay dolls – it's a very ancient witchcraft rite, for getting rid of undesirable people, or dangerous ones.'

He changed the subject. He picked up a toy car he had been

handling. It was a model of a Volvo.

'Have you noticed there aren't any red-haired boys at the school?'

She hadn't.

'Of course if the cult demands a victim, as you suggest, every five years, of course that's the lifetime of each school generation, and there aren't any likely candidates available, it places a bit of a problem on the cult, doesn't it?'

She could see that, the whole thing was quite fascinating.

'But it has to kept "in the family" as it were. You see that, don't you?'

Yes she did, it was all very obvious.

He smiled at her.

She heard the door open behind her and someone entered the room.

The Chaplain spoke again.

'I'm glad you understand. It's important to understand. He smiled at the person standing behind her.

'Yes, Headmaster, I think we're ready for you now ...'

I do not like thee, Dr Fell,
The reason why I cannot tell;
But this I know, and know full well,
I do not like thee, Dr Fell.

II

The Ferryman

Come, lets to bed, says Sleepy-head. Tarry a while, says Slow

Judith sat in the waiting room of the surgery. She could hear
the hum of busy traffic in the street below. The window was
open but the light breeze only brought in more heat. She
wondered again why even the most expensive of London
offices seemed not to have air conditioning. Any consultant of
Desmond's standing would have far better offices in the States.

The inner door opened and a middle-aged couple came out.
Desmond smiled at her as he showed them through to the
outer door. He was always so impeccably smart, she thought.
He came back.

'Judith ...' He held her hand and gave her a fatherly kiss on
the cheek.

'I'm sorry to have kept you waiting. Do come in.'

He ushered her in to his consulting room. It so reflected the
man. It spoke of restrained good taste and, she noticed,
seemed cooler than the outer waiting room. Perhaps they had
just forgotten to have the air conditioning on out there.

She sat opposite him, waiting. He looked down at the folder
on his desk. It was closed. She waited.

'Judith ... I've known you and your sister for so long.' He
looked up. She couldn't tell what he was thinking. He had all
the hallmarks of the professional. There was no emotion in his
voice ... he was being gentle.

'And I know how close you are ...' He shrugged. 'Twins
usually are – but you ... We understand one another?' She
nodded. She was unable to speak. If it had been good news he
would have come out with it straightaway. Her mind wouldn't

accept what was beginning to become obvious. He wasn't saying ... Perhaps that was the way he showed his emotions. She studied his dark jacket.

'After separation Siamese twins always remain exceptionally close – as you are ...' She concentrated on his silk tie. She thought that they called that knot a Windsor.

'And through our common interests I think I've got to know you both – very closely.'

He was finding it hard to say.

'But we know – don't we – that the physical part of us isn't all there is to it ... through our work in psychical research. You understand that, don't you, Judith?'

She looked into his eyes. They were kind but there was no trace of hope in his thoughts.

'She's dying, isn't she?'

The voice didn't sound like her own. It seemed to come from far away.

He put his hand out across the desk but she didn't take it. It stayed there like some incomplete bridge between them.

'Yes, Judith. I'm afraid there is no doubt. We can do nothing more ... Sylvia is dying.'

Somehow the shock was not as great as she had feared. Maybe she had been preparing for it. Maybe she had known, deep inside, with a subconscious knowledge, the inner instinct she knew they both shared, of each other's every move and feeling. Even now she wondered whether Sylvia, eight miles distant across London, knew as she knew – felt the pain as she had felt Sylvia's growing malaise within herself.

She reached out to touch her mind, to love her. But he was speaking again.

'There are, I think, three or four months. We can do a lot with drugs. She won't feel pain ...' He was looking at her, but she was reaching across the bustling city to their flat. She found her, the pain of grief struck at her heart. She knew. Judith closed her eyes, to love her, to soothe her. But in the doing of that the realisation struck deep. Their time was drawing to its close. She had to break off from her sister. The grief of loneliness was too much. She couldn't cope with being alone, without the other's mind, without the other's thoughts and feelings and vitality. It wasn't possible!

He had got out of his seat and was standing by her, holding both her hands in his. She looked up at him through her tears.

'Judith, Judith, many suffer separation. You will learn to live … on your own.'

'No one knows what it's like. Desmond, can't you see – we are one person.'

He looked at her closely.

'Have you been communicating with her now?'

'Yes, yes of course – and she can't cope with it. Neither of us can exist without the other. Don't you see?'

He knelt by her side, holding her hands, stroking them, his eyes full. He was not unaffected.

He looked away.

'What is it?' she asked, suddenly caught by something in his mind.

'What is it that you are thinking?'

He looked up and smiled at her.

'It's impossible to hide anything from you, isn't it?'

She wiped her eyes with the back of her hand.

'Only when it's that dramatic – usually I can't tell – but then suddenly –'

She couldn't put it into words but it was something like hope.

He let her hand drop away and stood up walking a few paces across the carpet.

'It isn't hope, Judith – just something …' His voice trailed off; he sounded embarrassed.

'What is it?' She was in full command of herself again.

He passed a hand over his forehead. He still had his back to her.

'Please say "no" if you find this unacceptable.' He turned, searching her eyes. 'You will, won't you?'

'Yes, of course.' She sat upright, her hands in her lap – not daring to reach out to her sister, not daring to let her know of the glimmer that had been kindled.

He began to pace the floor. He found it hard to say what he was saying, but she could sense his excitement.

'I know how committed you both are to psychical research.' He stopped, looking at her. She nodded giving him permission to continue.

'Well, there's a man – a colleague of mine – you probably haven't heard of him, he fights shy of any publicity, even among people like ourselves, who are committed. His name is Smith – Maddon-Smith. He lives in the West Country.' He spoke quickly as if he wanted to get it all out before he could disappoint her.

'Look, Judith …' He came to her again and held her hands. 'I must repeat, even though I know it distresses you, before I go on I must repeat – Sylvia is terminally ill. There is no hope of her recovering.' He shook his head as he said the words.

'No hope?' She was not distressed but puzzled. She was sure there was something.

He let her hands go again and resumed his pacing. He seemed to summon up courage. He stopped by the fireplace and looked at her.

'Maddon-Smith is working on a psychical research project into Post Death Experience. It's been kept very quiet, but you could help him.'

She felt deflated. It wasn't what she had expected. It wasn't hope. She had been wrong, but she listened to him still. He came across the room kneeling again by her chair.

'I'm not asking you to get involved, I'm merely telling you about it. Please believe me, Judith. I respect and love you both too much to play stupid games. It's just this – that you two are the most highly developed telepaths recorded so far. Perhaps because of your having been Siamese twins this has greatly enhanced a latent ability – but your ability to communicate with one another has never been equalled.' He paused but she began to catch a glimmer of the possibility and she had been wrong to discount it. It did provide a hope. As the conviction grew the burden of grief so newly acquired began to lift. If it

were possible for her not to be totally alone, if they could still
be together ... in some way.'

'Maddon-Smith is a qualified physician. If you want to stay
with him he could make sure that everything was right for
Sylvia. She would be well cared for ... and if you agreed to this
experiment, who knows what benefits it would provide for our
work. Judith, it's a one in a thousand million opportunity to
explore ...' he paused ... 'what is beyond.'

*

The journey down had to be made in easy stages. It had taken
two months to settle things in London and Sylvia's health had
deteriorated. She was, as Desmond Rolloson had said, without
pain, but had a growing lethargy which made the simplest
manoeuvres for travel a difficult and protracted business.

Autumn had come early and there was a chill in the air. By
the afternoon of their arrival a sea mist had crept up the creeks
and inlets of the Cornish south coast, blanketing everything in
a clinging damp whiteness which made even Judith shiver as
she climbed out of the car. The hill was steep down to the Ferry
and although only a few hundred yards below, she could not
see the water from where she had pulled in opposite the inn.
The inn sign over her head creaked a little as she stood on the
steps to ring the bell. Large droplets of damp fell from the sign
with flat dank splashes on the flagstones at her feet.

The outside light came on and Dr Maddon-Smith stood in
the doorway, his assistant tall and bespectacled just behind his
left shoulder.

'Miss Marriott – how good to see you.' He looked past her
to the small blue car.

'We must get your sister in out of the cold, Jasper. Bring a
rug for the other lady, will you?' He scurried after her, she
opening the car door for the assistant to get good leverage on
Sylvia, wrapped as she was in heavy blankets. Judith collected
two of the cases from the car boot.

They were soon well settled in the inn sitting room. A large
open fire crackled and spat, warming them as they nestled into

deep comfortable armchairs. It was empty apart from themselves. 'Not many people here?' Judith commented as the
publican's wife brought them tea.

'No, dear. As soon as the season's over we shut up. It's only
the locals that come, and the doctor of course, for the beer.' She
gave the doctor an affectionate nudge with her elbow.

'Come wind, gale or fog he makes it over most evenings.'
Maddon-Smith, the doctor, held up a stubby finger.

'Only by the good offices of Douglas in the fog though, Mrs
Shaw.'

'That's true, dear. No one can navigate the creeks in fog like
our Douglas ... He's the ferryman, you see, and his father before
him.'

The doctor winked at the two younger women.

'I always know where Douglas is after opening hours. I only
have to phone across and he comes and picks me up ... the
journey back's not always so navigationally correct though, Mrs
Shaw.'

He smiled up at the big woman who trundled away chuckling
to herself. They could hear her repeating the joke to her
husband in the bar.

The doctor wasn't at all like Desmond: short, balding, and
putting on weight, he wore untidy tweeds and had an air of
genteel decay about him. Judith had been unimpressed at their
first meeting six weeks before, but Desmond had been glowing
in his praise of the man, and, slowly, over their several subse-
quent meetings both sisters had rather taken to him.

He sat on one side of the inglenook patting his jacket pockets.

'I'm sure I had my pipe somewhere ... ah yes ...' He inspected
the interior and began poking about in it with a key from his
keyring, puffing and blowing trying to clear it of extinguished
ash.

He paused for a moment, looking at them both.

'You mustn't be worried about this awful weather.' He
pointed over his shoulder with his pipe stem.

'Pretty dismal out there just now – but we have some fine
autumn weather down here, and the house has got its own

generator so it's pretty warm.' He smiled at Sylvia. 'No need to worry about cold or damp – you'll be as snug as a bug in a rug, as my old Dad used to say.'

He patted his pockets again looking for his tobacco pouch and then looked at Sylvia's face. 'Prefer if I didn't smoke, girl?'

Sylvia was paler than normal and was beginning to look drawn.

'If you don't mind, doctor. It's been a long day.'

He held a stubby hand up. 'No sooner said than done.' He thrust the pipe back into his pocket. 'Probably do my health good anyway!'

'Have we rooms here for tonight, doctor?' Judith was concerned for her sister's symptoms of fatigue.

'Certainly you have – and don't feel at all afraid to break up the party and be off to bed. Jasper and I will get Douglas to take us across later. It'll be clear by tomorrow and we'll come and get you in my boat. But there's no hurry. You have a good relaxing time. They serve a good breakfast here by the way – so make the most of it.

*

The next day dawned bright and clear, the wide waters of the creek reflecting a pale blue sky. Sylvia was enchanted by the view, the deep woods that ran down to the banks on each side. They could see the doctor's house from the window – white and low and backed by the great woods which were turning to gold and brown among the greens. It was near the water's edge on a promontory something around an eighth of a mile away overlooking the confluence of two wide creeks. It had its own landing stage, Sylvia noticed, and no apparent track inland.

She turned to her sister from where she sat by the window.

'What an enchanting place to choose to die.'

Judith sat down on the window seat, taking her sister's hands.

'Don't say that, Sylvia.'

Her sister smiled at her.

'Why not? That's what we're here for. My love, don't look so glum. We are on the edge of a great adventure, you and I;

together – not apart – that's what it's all for – together.'

Judith leant forward and held her.

'Not so tight. Remember I'm easily damaged now.'

She leant back on the window seat and her sister caressed her cheek.

'Don't worry, my love. It will be all right – you'll see.'

Her sister tried to smile. 'I wish I had your confidence.'

Sylvia feigned shock.

'Now who's going on this journey – you or me? It's supposed to be the explorers who get nervous, not the base camp with the radio!'

They smiled at one another – and Judith vowed inside herself to try harder, although she would have willingly been the one to go, and not be left behind.

The trip across the water was more hazardous than they had imagined, the doctor's boat well laden with all the possessions Sylvia had wanted around her at the end. She was far more frail than anyone had realised – and spent a restless journey in the boat, ashen and hollow-eyed, taking no real notice of her new surroundings. But the house was good, warm and comfortable, happily confounding Judith's worst fears of the rather shabby Maddon-Smith.

Sylvia's room was on the ground floor. It looked out on the confluence of the rivers, a view down between deep-sided wooded valleys towards the estuary, and the sea another two miles distant.

She had been able to sleep after their arrival and Judith had been quietly busy in the room arranging precious personal possessions, photographs and flowers to greet her sister when she awoke. She had come to, and was expressing her delight when the doctor arrived at the door with the offer of a light lunch. He brought it in and Sylvia was sat up in her bed so that she could see the view. The doctor had had a bed tray made especially and she ate what small amount she could. The doctor himself asked permission to join them and sat with Judith at the gate-legged table by the window.

'I don't know if this is the appropriate time, but I wondered if you would be interested in my plans.' He was courteous and obviously kindly. He, like Desmond, was aware of what tender ground he trod but they had discussed and agreed all the theoretical basis for their work. He now wanted to show them how he intended organising their preparation for the experiment.

Sylvia smiled at him and cast a glance at Judith.

'We would be delighted, Dr Maddon-Smith.'

He lifted a hand.

'You feel …?'

'Quite rested, thank you. Yes … we are both looking forward to what you have to show us.'

Judith felt a twinge of pain at what her sister said but she knew it was inside herself and not transmitted from Sylvia. Sylvia was convinced; her dedication to the project had been absolute from their first meeting with the doctor and Judith understood a little of why it was. Sylvia's last few days – and the days beyond that, however many there were to be – had purpose, and the gift of purpose to one who was dying was, Judith supposed, the greatest thing one could offer.

They had discussed all the ethical and emotional aspects with both doctors already, and had been given a general understanding of the theory behind Maddon-Smith's proposals, but now they were ready for their briefing. Now the work would begin in earnest.

He leant forward in his seat, his hands dropping between the knees of his baggy trousers.

'As you know the machine we will use is a modifcation of the ECG principle. I want you both to get used to it. It registers not just brain waves but that elusive agent of the mind's activity. Many, even in the medical profession, confuse the purely functional and physical organ of the brain with the essence of the person which resides not in the brain as such but in the mind.' He shook his hand dismissively.

'So many confuse the two. However, with this considerably modified machine and with your remarkable telepathic link, we will be able to trace the progress of the mind itself, though –' he looked a little wary of saying the words – 'through and beyond what we call brain death.' He paused. 'With both of you used to the technique of using the device I think we can be pretty certain to carry on your contact after ... afterwards.'

Sylvia smiled at him.

'Don't be worried about saying it, doctor. It is good for me to be able to actually achieve something through all this. Don't worry.'

He looked relieved and pushed a stubby finger down his collar and loosened it.

'Thank you, Miss Marriott, and may I say now what a great privilege I feel in you ...' He looked at Judith.

'In both of you being prepared to share this experience with me ... a stranger.'

Judith took control.

'Do go on, doctor. We would like to hear all you have to say about the process.'

He leant forward again – absolved of his dilemma – his eyes shone with enthusiasm for his project.

'We have had many experiments. Dr Rolloson has been involved in some – with tracing not just brain waves, but psychic energy, what I like to call the mind, or if you like, the soul. With these techniques we finally have the potential of overcoming the last great unknown. We have the chance to see beyond death itself – into post death experiences – the psychic energy or mind will be traceable through your corporate link into the machine. You, Miss Marriott, will be able to trace what it is your sister experiences as she travels beyond our physical reach.'

He sat further forward his hands clasped one in the other.

'Always, all down the ages before, death has been the great divide, our psychical research to date – however hard we've tried – falls short. In the final analysis it always falls short. But now – with your gifts – linked into this machine – we have a chance. It reverses everything, do you see?

'Before, we have always been fearful of the dead, departed spirits, non-physical beings. Ghosts have always frightened us, always had the upper hand, so to speak, because they travel beyond our sight, beyond our knowledge. Death has always had the great power of the unknown, but now we have the chance of reversing the process. It is *we* who will be able to see into their world and not just they into ours. Death has always seemed to be the last great failure of man. His final last ironic capitulation, but with this – with you – we can change the rules of destiny – we can actually *know* …'

The days went by. The work with the machines – and their link-up – was more arduous than Judith had expected. The doctor and his assistant made repeated trials of the same material. It was obviously necessary, but Judith worried for Sylvia's well-being as the constant tests and re-tests drained her energy away. The doctor would spend many days into the early hours analysing and re-running data through the computers that ran in conjunction with the machine itself and would come to Judith with searching questions about the images they had transmitted and received – about the shades of difference in the interpretation of words and thoughts.

The weather held good for their first few weeks, the sunlight dancing on the water, the sea birds settling and flying in their hundreds. The sisters were always glad of their breaks from the work, for they could stay in their room overlooking the expanses of light. The work itself was carried on in a room at the back of the house, a clinic white-painted windowless room excavated from the rock that rose as a wall behind the building. Judith had begun to hate the room, and the couch that stood waiting by the back wall; there was to be no sunlight for Sylvia's last moments. She would be brought into the sunless room and laid on the couch, to be strapped to the machine one last time – for how long? Judith had no idea how long after the event of death.

The temperature of the room could be lowered – and would be when the time came – to preserve Sylvia's physical remains for as long as possible. It was their link. The doctor himself admitted to not knowing how long the physical link could be maintained or how long the psychic transmissions could be plotted in the humming technology he had so slavishly created.

Occasionally Douglas would row across with letters and an interlude would ensue when they could be absorbed by the world they had left behind, but as time went on Sylvia began to be distant even from these events.

Some nights the doctor would declare a break and would go off across the river with Jasper to the inn. These were treasured by Judith, when Sylvia and she were alone together again. She craved for the moments – precious as she knew they were – when they would be in each other's company alone ... But Sylvia often slept during these times, awaking hours later to apologise that she had not been good company and Judith would put down the book she had been reading by the bedside and assure her sister that there was no need to be fretful, yet deep inside, shielded from her sister's penetrating mind, she would feel the grief of approaching loneliness again.

As the trees turned more golden and many leaves began to float down the waters in front of the house the mists returned. One night the doctor declared a stop and walked out into the hall to find that in the hours of their incarceration in the white room the mists had come up again.

It was the only time Judith heard him swear. He went to the telephone and called Douglas to take him across to the inn. Sylvia again suggested that Judith go with them to the inn. It would do her sister good she said, and anyway she was so tired she would only sleep and be bad company again.

Judith didn't want to go – not that she didn't thirst for another place to be – but that she wanted to stay as long with her sister as possible. But Sylvia prevailed and Jasper was commissioned to stay by her bedside. It shocked Judith to the heart to hear the doctor whispering to his assistant – if anything should happen – to phone immediately and Douglas would bring them back. She somehow hadn't realised it could be so imminent, but she calculated quickly. They had already been at the house for a month; their time was running out.

It was another week and two days before it happened. One afternoon Judith went to the bedside to see a change had overcome her sister. Her breathing was shallow, her complexion far paler. She rang for the doctor and reached out across the gulf to hold her sister. She met her and received comfort from deep inside the prone figure. They took her immediately to the white room and Jasper deftly strapped her to the couch placing the tapes over her head. Judith sat in the chair allotted to her, her knuckles whitening as she clutched the handholds. The doctor applied the tapes to her own head and she watched the dial needles jump into life. Sylvia's breathing was shallow and her thoughts, after the initial contact of comfort, became confused, snatches of their early life, their parents. The doctor poured over the technology adjusting dials and checking switches.

It was a long wait. Jasper brought coffee, but it remained untouched. The journey had begun.

The data print-out chattered as her respiration began to stagger. The more common medical aids began to signify the decline. Judith reached out across the void and held her sister's mind. It had begun to move away. She was taken with it – down and down she seemed to go – it had become colder and darker. She began to feel the fear.

The machine too registered the changes. The doctor looked at her.

'Cold ... darkness ...?' She nodded. He returned to de-coding what the machine read and then the end came. The conventional medical technology finished its bleeping, a long drawn out whine indicated cessation of heart and major organs, but still the machine chattered and still she followed her sister down the path she was treading – through darkness now – feeling her way beyond the light of life. Another hour ticked by on the electric wall clock. The doctor sat passive by the gentle tapping of the machine. Judith – her eyes closed – followed the footsteps downwards. There was no mental communication from Sylvia – no speech – but somehow Judith accepted that. The emotions she felt – and the sights she saw – but no word passed between them. Sylvia was intent on something else now ... a translucence – a rippling light. The machine began to chatter, but Judith was concentrating: a sound came to her, the sound of lapping – a lapping of water.

'What is it? What is it?'

The doctor was too excited, insistent. He demanded to know direct from her and not wait for his translation of the machine.

She could have cursed him at her elbow. He distracted her.

'Water ... it's water.'

'What's she doing?'

'Waiting – waiting by the edge of the water.'

'Try to speak to her.'

She flapped at him with her hand trying to get rid of his insistence. She must concentrate.

The machine began chattering again. She saw something moving on the water. It was murky and dark. A deep impenetrable mist lay over the waves – but something moved out there ...

Sylvia stood by the edge, her back to Judith – she, too, was concentrating on what it was in the water. A feeling of anticipation and Judith shared it.

And then she saw it. It was a boat. But the noise of the machine intruded, chattering noisily.

'What now? What do you see?'

He could not wait to know. He couldn't wait for the computer read out. He insisted on knowing.

'It's a boat – a boat coming through the mist ...' She watched, her attention again on the scene before her.

But his exclamation came from beside the chair.

'It's the Styx – Jasper – it's the Styx. The Greeks were right – it's the Ferryman ...'

But Judith's concentration was arrested by her sister. She moved – along the shore – awaiting the boat. She gesticulated to her sister but what was it she said? Judith could not make it out. She tried to get closer, but like a dream her feet were leaden.

She seemed to drag a great weight with her as she edged nearer her sister.

The boat had stopped a little off from the shore. Sylvia wrung her hands and gesticulated again. Judith couldn't make it out. Sylvia was waving at her ... no ... she was waving her away – back. No words; she wanted Judith to go back. Judith's eyes went out to the boat. It lay on the dark waves, half hidden in the mist, the ferryman settled at his oars.

Sylvia gesticulated again, turning to her sister, she was imploring her to be gone.

'She wants to go. I'm stopping her from going. I'm holding her back.'

The doctor was by her side.

'Don't let her go. You must go down to the boat with her. Don't let her go ...'

Her sister was begging her. The oarsman still sat at his oars, on the waves, washing the beach in the darkness.

'I can't – I can't.'

With a mighty effort Judith pulled herself away from the scene. She turned in her chair – pulling at the tapes on her head. They came loose – falling around her.

'I can't do it!'

'What are you doing?' The doctor almost screamed at her. 'You will destroy the whole project.' He grovelled on the floor picking up the discarded wires and flex.

She stood up, staggering across the room. 'I'm going – I can't stay. I'm sorry but I can't stay here doing this.'

She struggled to the door and wrenched it open. It was dark beyond the hall. It was evening already. She went to the door. Thick fog met her gaze.

The doctor came through the door to the white room.

'You can't leave the experiment now. We are so near.'

She was at the phone. She didn't think what she was doing. She just knew she had to get out. Get out and get away.

'Hello – Mrs Shaw. This is Judith Marriott. Could you ask Douglas to come over and pick me up ... Yes ... there's a heavy fog ... now ... thank you ... yes ... thank you ...'

The machine had started to chatter noisily – the doctor had rushed back into the room to supervise.

She couldn't go back in. She opened the front door.

The machine would do as well as she could. It wasn't

possible for her to go back, to hold her sister back. She began down the path to the quay.

The doctor called her from the front door. She could see him silhouetted against the yellow light – the fog swirling around him. But she heard the oars pulling too.

'Miss Marriott – you can't leave now.'

The boat was visible, coming out of the mist, and she was so thankful. It grounded on the gravel. She clambered in.

She heard another shout from inside the house – Jasper's voice.

'Doctor – come quickly – we're losing her ...'

And then the boat took her out and she could hear the water lapping, and the mist closing over the house.

The doctor had left the front door open – and the door into the white room. Fingers of white mist explored the house.

He stood over the silent machine. The body of Sylvia Marriott lay strapped to the couch but no flicker of activity came from any of the dials.

Jasper turned to him, desperate.

'There was a great burst of activity and then this. Have we lost her, doctor?'

There was a shout from outside, and a knock on the front door.

"Hello ... Hello ...'

The doctor ran the tickertape through his hands scanning the silent dials.

"Hello – is anyone at home?' The doctor looked up. Douglas stood framed in the door, his waders on.

'Yes, Douglas, what do you want?'

'Miss Marriott, sir. She phoned and she wanted to be taken across. Is she ready sir?'

The doctor frowned, the blank tape held in his hands.

'But she's gone. You picked her up just now. I saw her – getting into the ferry. Didn't you have someone with you?'

'No, sir – I've just arrived and there's no one with me.'

The doctor's face paled.

'But I saw her ... get in ... beside the Ferryman – and he had another passenger with him ...'

Come, let's to bed,
Says Sleepy-head;
Tarry a while, says Slow;
Put on the pan,
Says Greedy Nan,
Let's sup before we go.

III

The Secret Garden

Mary, Mary, quite contrary

They slowed to a walking pace as they looked at each building.
The house fronted onto the village street – its ivy-clad walls
and mullion windows. Some of the inset stonework looked
ecclesiastical, with arches and carving. It was obviously some
hundreds of years old.

The elderly man pulled on the hand brake.

'Here it is – Abbey House.'

He looked at his grand-daughter – she squinted up at him
through the hot sunshine.

'You can see why they fell in love with it.'

'May I get out? I want to see if that bell-pull works.'

Samantha climbed out and mounted the two stone steps
pulling at the brass handle. The door opened almost
immediately.

'Max, Samantha, how lovely. You grow more pretty every
time I see you, Samantha.' Her grandfather's friend ruffled her
hair.

'Shh, David. She gets enough of that already – she doesn't
need you telling her as well.' The old friends shook hands.

Max looked around.

'Retirement in deepest Wroxetshire suiting you then?'

'You know me; I've been waiting for this for forty years. Let
me help you with the case. It beats pathology in London, I can
tell you.'

Max looked up at the house.

'Muriel, it's perfect, really perfect, and no garden I see ...
that should suit you, David.'

David peered from behind the car.

'What's that you're saying about me?'

'No garden, David. What did you pay them to get rid of the garden for you?'

Max followed him with the small overnight bag.

'You know, I never thought David would make a countryman – all that weeding and mowing – but blow me here he is with the only house in the country with no garden!'

'Don't be too certain about that.'

They entered the cool of the house into the wide white panelled hall with its curved staircase. Beyond, glimpsed through the door at the end of the hall, was a crowded rose garden, shimmering in the summer heat.

The guests looked at one another.

'What's this?'

Max put the case down and advanced towards the door. Samantha followed him to admire the profusion of colour that lay beyond.

'Uncle David – it's beautiful!' A rose garden gave way to tier upon tier of all manner of country flowers, abundant with colour and the busy sounds of summer bees.

'A real old-fashioned cottage garden. But it's enormous – you wouldn't expect it from the front. I thought you'd have a courtyard or something.'

'It's the new reformed David, you see.' His wife smiled at him linking her arm through his.

'All his own work. The countryside has had its effect.'

'All this in six months?' Max sounded dubious; he smiled with disbelief. 'Come on, David. Even the houseplants I gave you in London died. You wouldn't know a green finger if it was sticking in your eye.'

His friend winked at him. 'We'll tell you later. Let's take you upstairs and when you've washed and had a look round the house we'll take you outside. It will be cooler then. You are the first real gardener we've had to show it off to.'

*

They sat in the low ceilinged drawing room, the double french windows open into the banked garden. Tea had been spent with animated approval of the roses that filled the room and the house, a very particular kind that Max had not seen before.

'They really are exquisite, aren't they? Miss Hobswynd – oh I must tell you about Miss Hobswynd. She says they're her own creation and guards them with her very life. She calls them the Novice Rose. It's because of the dark ring around the light centre, like a Novice Nun, you know ...'

'They're amazing.' Max lifted one out of the bowl on the table, inspecting it at close quarters.

'It's just like a little face. Look do you see? The dark eyes and mouth and cheekbones.' He turned it one way and then another. 'Just like a young girl in a wimple, with all this dark gathering around it. Extraordinary.'

'And you say she cultivated this strain herself? It's astonishing she's never exhibited it. I've never seen anything like it ... I'd love a cutting. Do you think I dare ask this woman of yours?'

'I wouldn't if I were you, she'll probably get angry and turn you into a toad ...'

'David!' His wife sounded cross. 'Don't say things like that, she can't help being a little odd, the more people say it the more everyone will think it.'

Her husband smiled to himself but remained silent.

'We must show you the garden.'

'Ah yes ...'

'You were right, of course; we were looking for something without a garden.'

His wife interrupted:

'It was incredibly difficult – finding what we particularly wanted; near the sea, but not too near and a house of the size we wanted without a garden. We looked all over the place.'

Her husband scowled at her interruption and continued:

'As I was saying ...' She let him tell the story. 'It was actually something of a mistake us getting it. The estate agent stupidly didn't mention the garden and – of course – the house is just what we were looking for, but the garden horrified us.'

'I knew it! I told you so!' Max held up a finger, vindicated.

'We said this to the people who were selling and they said that they were not gardeners either; the whole thing was done for them, by some little old woman, Miss Hobswynd, who lives in the cottage.' He turned to look out of the window. 'You can't see it from here, but it must originally have been part of these buildings. It was all a nunnery – pre-Reformation. It was attached to Silchester Abbey – that's our nearest town. But that was all – her house and this are the only bits of it left apart from the church – that's the other side of her cottage.'

His wife interrupted again.

'It's a funny arrangement of buildings. You'll be able to see when we go out, but the garden is entirely enclosed by the two houses and the back of the church and the high old garden wall which must have been the original cloister. It was probably the old nunnery garden. It's got a kind of "secret garden" quality ...'

Her husband coughed and continued.

'Anyway, Miss Hobswynd has looked after it for years, since before the last people moved in apparently; and that was nearly forty years ago. She's a funny old dear really – goodness knows what age she is – one of your green-fingered old country folk. I've caught her talking to the plants before now ... But she enjoys it, so it doesn't trouble us.'

He looked at his wife, expecting an interruption.

'Yes – you mustn't mind Miss Hobswynd.' She leant forward a little lowering her voice in a confidential kind of way. 'I don't think she likes people much at all. The plants are her friends, she says ... She's a bit odd, comes in occasionally to complain about me cutting things for the house ... that sort ...'

'Oh come off it, Muriel. You're making her sound worse than she is. It's probably living alone all these years so near to the graveyard. No one from the village ever goes near her cottage, and I think the village children are a bit frightened of her. They call her a witch, which is a bit unkind.'

'Well, she doesn't help her image much, does she, darling? I've been over there a couple of times when she's making her potions ... believes in herbal cures and things – not exactly eye of toad, but some pretty whiffy brews.'

She stopped. Her husband had just touched her arm. A shadow had fallen across the carpet near one of the open windows.

'Miss Hobswynd, is that you?' He called with raised voice, as if speaking to someone deaf.

There was silence for a moment. They all looked towards the window, the sunlight falling through it. The shadow on the carpet moved again, and suddenly there she was. Samantha gave a gasp; she certainly was a quite extraordinary figure, small and wide with an enormous dark hat clamped to her head, white gloves and a long patterned frock. She held a rug over one arm with vegetables in it, and in one hand a crumpled brown paper bag.

She didn't speak to anyone in the room but Samantha, and advanced upon her.

'Oh I thought you had a little girl here – and so pretty. Would you like a sweet, my pretty one?'

She proffered the paper bag. Samantha visibly cringed into her seat, shaking her head.

'These are my special ones, not for grown-ups, just for young ones, like ye and me.'

She was now by the side of her chair holding out the open bag.

'You have one, my pretty, and then you'll know you've got a friend in Miss Hobswynd.'

Her teeth were uneven, some blackened and some missing. It was no wonder the villagers were frightened of her. She placed the bag by Samantha's side.

'I'll leave them here for you, my little one.' She suddenly extended a surprisingly long finger, pointing at Samantha's face.

'But don't let any of them have them, oh no, these be special, just for ye and me.' She turned on her heel, dropping the rug of vegetables on the polished side table. As she did so clods of earth fell on to the floor.

'Some carrots from the garden,' she announced, and was gone as quickly as she came.

Their host looked concerned at his grand-daughter's expression but she seemed to relax as the old woman left the room and almost absent-mindedly picked up the brown paper bag.

'Are you all right, my dear?'

'Yes, of course, Grandpa.' She sounded very definite. Her grandfather was reassured.

'That was Miss Hobswynd.' David was apologetic.

'Yes, I'm afraid she's a bit like that.'

'Not too many social graces,' his wife added.

'You can say that again. What a weird old lady!'

'She's not really all that bad – just a bit ... eccentric.'

'I don't think you ought to have those sweets, my dear.' Her grandfather moved across to collect them, but the girl tightened her grasp upon them, holding them to her chest, uncharacteristically defiant.

'They're mine, Grandpa.' Her grandfather stopped, arrested in her movement.

'Yes, of course, my dear. But I don't think ...'

'Oh, do let her have them, Max. The old girl's quite harmless really, just dotty. How about this trip round the garden then?'

*

The praise of the garden turned to astonishment as they moved from the flower beds through an ancient arch into an enclosed section between the church and Miss Hobswynd's cottage.

'This is quite incredible. You've got some amazingly rare species here – things one wouldn't expect to see outside Kew.'

Max advanced upon a curiously shaped specimen.

'Do you realize what this is? It's a living Mandrake. They're supposed to be extinct. The story goes that they scream if you pull them up.'

'I think Miss Hobswynd is more likely to scream if you tried.'

'But it's quite incredible, fascinating. Some of these plants were used in mediaeval medicines. I must look them up when I get home ... And these are positively venomous. Don't go near them, Samantha. Keep your hands away. Is that possibly a Venus Fly Trap? It's gigantic. Big enough to eat small birds, I should think.'

Max tore his eyes away from the curiously shaped plant life that so fascinated him.

'This is a remarkable find. Have you any idea how rare these things are?'

His host shook his head.

'I've never taken any real interest in it, Max. We don't normally come to this part. It was the old kitchen garden, I think. Miss Hobswynd has this part.'

'He has his time cut out identifying Canterbury Bells and hollyhocks, let alone Mandrakes.' His wife had no illusions about his horticultural expertise.

'You must be right about its origins though. This was probably the herb garden, it must have been here all that time.'

'But tended by whom?'

Their guest pondered the question.

'It's just not possible for them to have survived without continuous care. It must have been handed on, from one generation to another. I'd love to ask Miss Hobswynd ...' He moved on. 'I don't even recognise some of these. They must be compatible in date with the Mandrake back there, but I'd have to look them up. Do you realise these are probably unique?'

'Well, I'm glad you find it fascinating.' David was obviously beginning to tire of the slow progress. 'I'm sure Miss Hobswynd would be delighted to talk. I'm afraid she doesn't get much enthusiasm out of us. This is her cottage, by the way. This is the blank side. You see where the old windows have been walled up?'

'Pity she hasn't got an outlook over the garden.'

'Yes. I suppose it was done when the nunnery buildings were divided. Her windows all overlook the graveyard. Pretty dismal really, and the church blocks her view of the village so she's only got graves to look at.'

'Oh, but there aren't many of those, darling. That's the

north side of the church. They only bury suicides on the north side.'

Max looked up from where he was inspecting an exotic bloom.

'What a particularly miserable prospect, but I don't suppose there are many of those in a village this size.'

'Well, funnily enough there do seem to be quite a lot – even recently. Over the past twenty years or so there have been a couple. I read their headstones one afternoon. They all seemed so young, poor things. Just goes to show it's not just nowadays that there are problems. I expect most were lovers' tiffs or something; young girls doing away with themselves because of cruel men!'

'You make us sound like beasts. I can't see any young girls killing themselves for you or me, can you, Max?'

'Speak for yourself, old man. I've still got some zest in me you know.'

The hosts finally drew him into the house. Samantha had long got bored and wandered back to sit in the drawing room.

*

The evening ran on, Samantha went to bed but conversation kept returning to the garden and its astonishing plants.

'Really, David, it's quite amazing that they should have survived for so long. I wonder how they did?' He posed the question for the eighth or ninth time.

His host idly tampered with the paper bag by his side.

'Miss Hobswynd would be bound to know. She's been here for donkey's years.' He paused as his fingers explored the opening of the bag. He peered inside.

'Do you want a sweet?'

At least it changed the conversation which he felt was becoming more than tedious.

He offered the bag to Muriel.

'Darling, you shouldn't. Miss Hobswynd gave them to Samantha.' His wife was a stickler for such proprieties.

He ignored the comment, sniffing the aroma.

'They smell delicious. Come on, Max, have one?' He took the bag and looked inside.

'He's right. They smell just like an old candy shop.'

He took one out and put it into his mouth.

'That takes me back ...' He closed his eyes and settled back on the sofa.

'I haven't tasted anything like that since I was a boy.' He looked up,

'Do try one, Muriel.'

David handed the bag to his wife who took from the bag a bright yellow powdered sphere.

'They really are very good.'

The sweets were a success.

'Samantha really ought to have the last three. After all they were given to her to eat,' Muriel muttered.

The two men were slightly abashed at their self-indulgence.

'Quite, Muriel, quite. But, still, we would each have had three if we leave these for her.

To the disgust of the host the evening didn't pass without a reintroduction of the subject of Mandrakes and other plants. In flight from the subject of plants their host was even prepared to launch into questions about the pathology laboratory and its staff, a subject that didn't really interest him in his retirement. But his guest, having been his second in command for years, had taken over control after his retirement and was obviously doing very well – which was pleasing, but only worth airing in preference to the dreaded subject.

Finally they retired to bed, prepared for a good night's rest.

The next morning was heralded with bright sunlight which promised another hot day. The windows of the breakfast room thrown open early already admitted a warm breeze into the house, but only Samantha seemed pleased with the day. The adults all wore slightly languid expressions – evidence of a disturbed night, and the question of sleeping well was met with a half-hearted response. Their host was more to the point.

'If it was anything like my night it was awful.' The others looked up.

'Well, to tell the truth, old man – I have spent more relaxing nights.'

'It was the awful dreams.' Muriel agreed she, too, had been disturbed by horrible nightmares.

'It was all your damn talk about Mandrakes that got me.'

'Plants – I have to suffer them all evening and get them invading my sleep as well!' David's experiences had not entirely robbed him of his resentment of the previous evening.

'How extraordinary. Mine was about plants as well, and that awful Miss Hobswynd.'

'So was mine ...'

Samantha sat eating her breakfast nonchalantly uninterested in the conversation of her elderly partners.

'I wasn't going to mention it, but it does seem odd – all dreaming the same kinds of things.'

'Was yours about ...' Max paused, he looked slightly embarrassed. 'This sounds silly ... but about plants screaming?'

The others assented. A coincidence.

'And ...' he paused again, seeming unwilling to confide, his fear of the night seeming foolish in the sunlit room. 'About Miss Hobswynd ...' He paused a third time. 'Hopping about.' The others agreed.

'Yes – it sounds stupid, doesn't it? – but it was like prancing rather than hopping and laughing, and talking to the plants, getting nearer, and then further away. It was ... terrifying ... and her face, all white with perspiration, grinning with those rotten teeth.'

Muriel stopped her husband's flow with a pressure on his arm. Samantha was present and would be frightened by such talk.

But it was extraordinary that their dreams should be the same. The conversation lapsed until the two men were alone.

'You know, David – I've been thinking about those nightmares.'

'So have I.'

They were standing leaning against a small bridge by the local inn.

'It wasn't the conversation, was it?'

'No, it wasn't. But I've got a horrible notion of what it might have been.' He looked up at his friend.

'Those sweets?'

'Precisely what I thought.' He looked away, down at the stream flowing peacefully below them.

'Thankfully we've still got some. May I take them to the lab – I'd like to do some analysis?'

'I'd appreciate that, Max. I was going to suggest the same, but I'd prefer not to let Muriel know. It would spoil her relationship with the old girl. I think Muriel's the only friend she's got in the village. And it's only a surmise, of course. All the same, I think you had better keep little girls away from your Miss Hobswynd until we've worked this one out.'

'That's precisely what I thought – but we're not likely to get many young female guests at our age. The grandchildren are all older than that now, so I think that might be safe. Teenagers aren't really into sweets.'

'It might even be a case for the police.'

David was perturbed at the thought.

'I do hope not. She's a harmless enough old biddie. She probably got the recipes muddled or something.'

'But if that were true – just thinking for a moment – whatever was it that the sweets were meant to induce? Can you imagine the effect of one person eating all of them?'

*

The letter from his friend came at the same time as another bearing more weighty family news, and so probably didn't get the attention it deserved.

On recollection afterwards David realised he hadn't even mentioned the letter to Muriel, but it probably wouldn't have made any real difference to the outcome … things being as they were.

He gave it a cursory glance. The contents of the sweets were highly toxic, an extraordinary compilation. Two passages came back to him afterwards: 'It's precisely the kind of concoction that one reads about from the days of witchcraft. They used to fill their candidates with this stuff before they had their hallucinatory rides on broomsticks.' 'Goodness knows what effect it would have had on Samantha had she eaten all of them.' But that was all afterwards.

The other letter was addressed to his wife and came from their eldest daughter who was having a very difficult time with their eldest grandchild having been sent down from university. Their daughter blamed herself; having had a nomadic life with her husband being in the army her children had never really had a settled home. But it was all too much – and such was the reputation that the granddaughter had now acquired she couldn't possibly stay on the army camp with them any longer. Drugs, boys, parties. It would be impossible to have a senior officer's daughter running around with all the private soldiers. Could she come to stay for a few months? She had always so adored her grandparents – and their home was the only one she had ever really known.

It was the kind of letter that both sent the recipients into paroxysms of uncertainty, but they couldn't refuse.

Susan arrived the following week and seemed to settle in well. It was true that she had always got on well with her grandparents, who were quietly critical of their army son-in-law's approach to his children. They suspected he was too repressive for the likes of Susan. They were, too, perhaps a little smug that it was into their care the girl had been placed, her parents having failed.

Susan settled in well, and struck up an immediate relationship with Miss Hosbwynd. They spent many hours in each other's company.

The grandparents' pride and pleasure were increased further as the days of autumn drew in and they could report weekly to their daughter and her husband that under their supervision Susan had taken to gardening and had even began to make preserves of garden produce. She had begun to enjoy embroidery and was working on a sampler in the evening. Her grandmother enjoying penning the message: 'She positively shuns television or any of what she now describes as "twentieth-century time-wasting" and spends hours enjoying simple old-fashioned pursuits.'

Some weeks later she was even able to write – with a degree of grandmaternal exultance:

Susan joined the church choir for the first time this week. She looked so sweet in her cassock and choir hat. Quite angelic – just like a young nun.

But as the mists of November rose among the skeletal remains of the garden the terrible thing happened. The thing that changed their lives. For no apparent reason Susan had got up early one morning and left the house. She hadn't even dressed but had gone from the house in her nightdress and had somehow gained access to the church.

She had climbed the tower and toppled over the parapet. It was a terrible tragedy. The grandparents – so proud of their work with her – were grief-stricken.

There was the question of suicide – or even murder. The police asked questions but there was no evidence of anything but some appalling accident.

At the funeral in the church the vicar spoke of the sadness which had again visited the parish. Yet another young life lost. On the insistence of her parents she was laid to rest in the village churchyard. They thought it right as it was the only real 'home' she had known, unlike the characterless cemeteries of the army camps she had known.

Her grandmother was upset that the grave should be on the north side. She said that that was for suicides, but the vicar assured her that that was no longer the practice and it was merely practical as there was no more room for burials on the south side. She was heartened and said that at least Susan would be under the eye of her new-found friend Miss Hobswynd. Her husband, however, did not appear pleased with the notion, and would not speak of it.

He became increasingly brooding as the weeks passed and

would often visit his grand-daughter's grave. His wife followed him once, and watched him from a distance as he knelt beside it, not in prayer but somehow studying the ground. He lay full length and eyed the level of the new earth mound, as if he expected some change.

And the winter came and snow blanketed the soil, but still he would venture out, sometimes at night, and conceal himself by the churchyard wall overlooking the desolate little grave as if he were waiting for something.

The silence would be long in their evenings, the ticking of the clock the only noise, and he would suddenly get up and leave, going, she knew, to his strange solitary vigil watching over the grave of their grandchild.

Miss Hobswynd too had changed her manner, moving about still more stealthily. Some mornings, very early, before the low lying winter sun tinged the sky, Muriel would hear a quiet muttering in the garden, and it would be Miss Hobswynd talking to the dormant plants, or digging curious little trenches around them in the cold earth, and bending near them, whispering.

*

One afternoon in early January Muriel suddenly grew tired of the oppressive silence of the house and she determined to visit the old woman. She walked out into the grey churned slush of the wet snow and across the garden. On entering her small courtyard she was repelled by the smells emanating from the house. Steam rose in large damp clouds on the cold air and around the kitchen windows. The windows themselves were covered in moisture, the smell appalling, repellent, and Muriel was about to turn away on the threshold when she heard the voice from within. A chanting, half singing voice of Miss Hobswynd. She crept closer, intrigued to see if she could glimpse inside the room, and suddenly to her terror the old woman's face appeared pressed at the window, round and white with perspiration running down the cheeks, her rotting teeth set in a wide grin.

'Hello, dearie,' she called out – too loud. 'Come to see me then?' Muriel was uncertain, unnerved by the sudden appearance – half choked by the stench.

'Come in, dearie – don't mind the mess.'

She was drawn, unwillingly into the oppressive little room heavy with the clinging clouds of moisture which rose in great rolling waves from the enormous bubbling cauldron. The thick liquid seethed with the heat, green globules of fat bubbling against the thick scum on the top. Muriel had never seen a real old cauldron before but what was in it, filling it to its brim, she had no idea.

She recovered from her fright, fighting against the nausea of the confined space and terrible stench.

'What are you doing?'

Miss Hobswynd seemed lighthearted, moving about the small space with amazing dexterity for an elderly person, vigorously stirring the thick bubbling liquid or arranging canisters on the shelves beside the boiler.

'It's special compost, dearie. Not many knows about Old Mary's special brew. It's for plants – my little ones. This time of year they need the extra nourishment before the spring; it's what keeps them going. I makes up a batch that lasts some years – I'd got very low, but this batch'll do fine now. They'll be happy now. That's why they thrived all these long years. I know their secret likings; they tell me, see.'

She laid a greasy finger against her nose and winked through her matted hair.

She was a weird old woman but even in such extraordinary circumstances Muriel was somehow enchanted by her almost pantomime eccentricity. She could see why the villagers thought her a witch. For the first time in months – in these strange surrounds – Muriel felt more at ease. In the company of a crazy old woman who listened to what the plants wanted to eat, she suddenly felt as if she shared something of the old woman's elation.

She asked the question quite aimlessly – to make conversation really:

'How long have you been looking after them?'

The old woman peered at her through her grimy hair and stirred the cauldron. She whipped a greasy hand through her hair and creased up one eye as she tried to think.

'Oh ... around six hundred and fifty years, I should think by now, my dear.' And she laughed an uproarious howling laugh. It was that laugh more than the comment that unnerved her. Miss Hobswynd was just a mad old woman, but Muriel's peace of mind had suddenly vanished and she wanted to be away, even if it was only to the silence of David's morose company. At least he was ... human.

She got back to the house through the cold air but she could still smell the stench clinging to her clothes, inside her nostrils. She felt she needed a good hot bath. She came in through the back door just as her husband was entering from the front. He was wide-eyed and pale. He tore his scarf off and then his jacket – he was beside himself.

'Whatever's wrong? David, you look dreadful, dear. What's wrong.'

'She's done it – I've been waiting for this – but she's done it. God alone knows what she is, but by the name of God I'll stop her.'

'Whatever do you mean? Who – who are you talking about?'

'That hag in the cottage. I should have reported it months ago, but it was too preposterous – I couldn't believe it myself. Even after Max's letter – even after poor Susan's death – even with those damned Novice roses of hers. It's all so obvious but I couldn't make myself believe it. I didn't want to believe it, but I'll stop her – whatever she is.'

She held him, forgetting the stench on her clothes, forgetting her own afternoon. She didn't understand his ranting, but she felt he had come back; he was speaking, sharing, she would only hold him while all his rantings came out.

'My love – can I do anything? Sit down, tell me what it is.'

She led him to the drawing room and he sat quaking in her arms.

'She's dug her up.'

'What do you mean, my love? What are you saying?'

'She's dug her up – Susan – her body's gone – and that thing at the end of the garden has done it. It was she that killed her – and she's dug her up.'

Muriel couldn't grasp the meaning: his silence all this time, his obsession with watching the grave, and now this incredible accusation ... She desperately tried to fit it together, but she felt there was a piece of the jigsaw missing. None of it made sense. It was all incredible and confused. David had been pushed too far by the events that had overtaken them. He suddenly straightened, more himself.

'I must phone Max and get him down here. Max will help.' He looked at his watch.

'It's only five o'clock now. He would be here in three hours if he left immediately. Eight o'clock – nine more likely.'

He moved out of her arms – purposeful – to the phone in the hall. Five minutes later he was back, stalking the room, silent again, but different, determined. She still couldn't understand, but she would wait.

Max arrived much later than David had hoped. David had been uncommunicative again all evening so she had left him in his brooding silence and had gone to have her bath. Afterwards she sat by one of the bedroom windows, thinking. She didn't know how long she had sat thus, in unseeing thought, but she was suddenly aware of a movement in the garden. She stood at one of the bedroom windows and there, on the far side of the garden, was Miss Hobswynd. By the light of a bright and cold three-quarter moon Muriel watched the stooped shrouded figure. She looked as if she was tilling the frozen ground around the rose bushes with a curiously shaped white stick – but then Muriel realised she wasn't tilling, but placing the white stick in the ground, pushing it down into the earth where she had previously dug the trenches.

Muriel watched her from a concealed place behind the

curtains. The old woman wandered to and fro talking, crouching and occasionally going to the container, one of the many Muriel had seen that afternoon, and tipping it up, the thick liquid running out into the trenches. It looked almost like jelly from where Muriel stood.

It was then that she heard Max ring the door bell. She realised they'd talk long into the night, but she could go to bed. David would be safe with his old colleague in the house. She got undressed and into bed pondering all she had heard and seen yet not understood. She didn't understand the accusation or references to a letter from Max however much she went over it. Finally she fell asleep as she thought, no nearer a conclusion that would make sense of David's fury and then his silence again.

*

The day dawned clear and bright. Hoar frost stood out sharp and sparkling on the trees in the garden. Muriel was awake first and stood by the windows. She noticed how much of the soil had been disturbed in the garden. Miss Hobswynd must have been working long into the night, presumably by moonlight, to have finished her work. Muriel stood wondering about the puzzle she had left the night before. Perhaps Max would enlighten her. She hoped he would call her to one side and suggest visiting a specialist. It would be too terrible to think of David having a breakdown when he had so longed for the relaxation of retirement. She looked over to the other bed where he lay asleep, looking so peaceful.

Over breakfast she mentioned the cauldron of the afternoon before, and the men exchanged grim looks, but said not a word to her.

She watched them as they donned the boots and the overalls Max had brought in his car. The shovels and plastic bags of his trade lay in neat rows by the garden door. The yellow wooden case of phials and glass bottles she remembered so well were brought out, but there were additional objects as well. Two silver crucifixes lay among the paraphernalia of the pathologist, and a large glass bottle with the label 'Sulphuric Acid'. But they told her nothing of the preparations, merely carrying things to and fro and telling her to keep inside with the windows and doors locked.

They went into the garden, and once they had seen her lock the garden door, they took the bottle of acid and began to pour it in steaming rows along the sides of the rose bed. She watched them, fascinated, as they turned from this to digging around the first rose bushes where the night before Miss Hobswynd had been carefully tending her prized 'friends'.

Muriel stood at the window at a loss to understand their vandalism; the old lady would be horrified.

They dug deep and the first bush began to quiver. She saw her husband take hold of it and pull, his legs apart straining. She could see the roots begin to pull out and then the ear-piercing scream as it came out of the ground. She could hear it distinctly through the closed window. The sound of the scream had riveted her to the spot, but neither of the men seemed hurt. And then she saw the roots of the plant twitching and convulsing; it had been the plant that screamed. The men took no notice, as if they had expected it; they were too busy already involved in another activity, burrowing in the root cavity, and began pulling something out of the ground. At first she recognised it as one of the white sticks Miss Hobswynd had buried, but with their gloves carefully wiping it over, the earth came off to reveal a bone – a long bone. She recognised it immediately. After years living with a pathologist it wasn't hard to recognise a human femur. They laid it down carefully and foraged again. A larger, spherical object came to the surface. Muriel could tell what it was before the earth was scraped clear, a human skull. They lay it next to the bone they had already excavated and began attacking the next bush.

Muriel looked up the garden, by instinct rather than by sight she knew of the old woman's approach.

She had never seen anything so disfigured with rage as the ball of fury that swept down the garden at the two men, her face a mask of unutterable horror the old woman rushed at them spitting with venom, her eyes green and glaring like a cat's. She halted, her long-fingered hands up to her face as both men simultaneously lifted their arms to her. They held small silver objects in their hands, holding them out against her and she began to circle them, not like an old woman at all; the tattered clothes hung not from the wasted limbs of a little old lady, but rather lean and powerful limbs, like the limbs of some animal about to pounce.

She circled them hissing and spitting, her eyes huge, turning from green to yellow, her hands long talons, hooked nails scratching at them and backing away as she circled, passing Muriel standing in the window, circling them, waiting to jump.

Max picked up the bone with one hand and waved it shouting at her. Muriel couldn't catch what he said, all the time holding the crucifix towards her in his other hand.

David snatched at the rose bush, its roots still feebly twitching and threw it at their assistant. She let out a howl of anguish as the dying bush brushed her clothing. Max swung the bone, hitting another of the rose bushes and shouted another speech at her – long words – hard to understand – but rehearsed. Muriel could see they had planned all this attack. The rose bush snapped, white sap spurting into the air like some colourless blood from a slashed artery.

The long limbed hag screamed in anguish, writhing, her talons imploring rather than menacing. David hit another of her plants with his spade, felling it, and she fell to her knees reaching out her long-taloned limb, the other hand clutching at her throat. The rose bed behind them began to smoulder as the effects of the acid permeated the roots, the plants beginning the topple against one another, the air rent with screeching.

Suddenly it was over, the heap of clothing that had been the old woman lurched and coughed and collapsed into itself, decaying before their eyes into a dark rich mass of matted hair and pulp which bubbled and spluttered and began to run away in rivulets back into the ground. Around them the garden of neat frosted rows began to convulse and stagger, a fruit tree toppled over, pulling out of the ground. January frost steamed as the ancient garden began to die.

*

It took many days to excavate the whole of the rose garden, but Max was able to use his influence to call in a large team from the pathology laboratory.

The bones were all human; they assembled nineteen full skeletons, all of them young females, some of quite considerable age, but one very recent, still with some of the boiled sinews clinging to the separated joints.

'God knows how long it had been going on ... some kind of medieval coven, I suppose. The nunnery could never really have been Christian; it was the ideal cover in those days.' Muriel sat down by his side, her hand resting on his knee.

Max looked up from the fire.

'I've looked the name up. Did I tell you? *Hob* is old English for the devil – *Wynd* means friend. It's obvious really, she was Sister Mary Hobswynd.' David didn't really listen – he looked back into the flames.

'They'd been using young novices before of course, to keep the garden growing, their boiled remains.' His voice caught.

Max spoke away from him following his own train of thought.

'We'll have to get the graves on the north side of the Church exhumed, of course, but there won't be any bodies.'

David's eyes looked tired, searching the flames.

Mary, Mary, quite contrary
How does your garden grow?
With silver bells and cockle shells,
And pretty maids all in a row.

IV
Déjà Vu

There came a big spider ...

'Have you ever wondered why people don't like spiders, Michael? It seems an absurd dislike really. They do so much good, clearing our homes of unwanted intruders; yet there is this sort of detestation people have of them. Perhaps it's their intelligence that unnerves us – do you think – the way they seem to calculate the death of their victims; it's almost a human trait, don't you think?' The younger colleague took a deep breath, but remained silent. His companion continued, undeterred:

'The tensing of their long legs, the sudden scurrying, darting movement of their traverse across their webs. Their sudden appearance on the edge of a desk when one is working late at night, or on a bedroom wall as one is just about to extinguish the lamp before sleep. The fear that there might be one there, unobserved, but waiting until we are unconscious, do you think? I've heard that some psychiatrist has tried to analyse it; he explained it as a subconscious reaction to the habit they have of keeping their prey hanging ... The dead remains of their consumed victims festooning the nest – fragile, empty decorations sucked dry of their life, witnesses to meals of the past, for those others, half alive, half dead, paralysed victims waiting until their host chooses to scamper towards them and sink its teeth into their quivering flesh, to suck out the life.'

Michael remained unmoved, his older colleague was enjoying himself too much to be stopped.

'Have you ever imagined the sight of the six eyes of the spider unblinking close at hand, watching you as the pain

73

increases and you hear the sucking noise of its repast, and feel your life draining away?'

Michael remained silent, gently tapping his pencil into the palm of one hand. For Michael Muffet there was a more tangible reason for the dislike that his colleague had so enjoyed. Ever since some stupid teacher at his prep school had demanded that he play Little Miss Muffet in a school concert he had loathed the mention of spiders. He didn't fear them – or so he told himself – but to be plagued as boys will be, by the same nickname all through his prep-school days was enough he felt for anyone. He had hoped to escape it, but it had followed him with several of his classmates to his public school and even on to university.

And now, even in a purely academic pursuit studying feudal culture, it had arisen again. He tried to contain himself as his fellow historian chuckled with well-worn mirth.

'Of course, Michael, you'll have to put up with his spiders. I hope it doesn't spoil your meals. Not that the Pingle is likely to serve up curds and whey, of course!'

'No, of course not.' He was determined not to rise to the bait.

He wrote down the address, the far west of Wales, without even a phone. That he felt would be vile enough, even forgoing the spiders.

'You're amazingly lucky the old boy has invited you down – he's quite a recluse. But it's the best possible opportunity. One of the only truly feudal systems still in existence. I expect it's your name that got you in, him being an arachnidologist?'

Michael returned a cold smile.

'I suppose there are other landowners who still run their estates like that, but even the Scottish lairds are losing people to the cities. It's amazing that the estate workers still stay ...' his colleague ruminated on. Michael assembled the notes he had made and checked the address again. He began thumbing through the tomes of train and bus timetables.

'It's frightfully out of the way – even more so with the cutback on local bus services. I believe one of the servants will be picking you up from the nearest market town. That's the end of the public transport system – about eighteen miles from Llyspingle on the edge of the estate.'

'How big is the estate?'

'Oh, God knows.' His colleague checked the old estate map. 'In the 1880's when this was last updated it stretched for miles – a good deal of mountain and forested valley of course. Not very profitable land.'

'But it hasn't been carved up by death duties?'

'Well, that's the odd thing. I haven't been able to find any records of his father's death or his own birth for that matter. They must have them at Somerset House of course.' He looked up some notes. 'The census information shows a static population for years. Longevity appears to be the thing in that part of the world.'

Michael shrugged. It didn't signify anyway. He would be able to explore all that when he got there, assuming the parish records were extant.

'They seem almost self-sufficient on the estate. I'd love to come with you. It's a real gem, something from another age. But I've got all this data from the National Trust to go through. That'll take a week or two at the least.'

*

The journey had indeed been a long one; the main line train from London, then the wait, and the single track local train through the valleys, up through the dismal villages, again a wait, and then the jolting wheezing bus-ride. The mountains glowed through the drizzling rain, the damp silent passengers diminishing in numbers until he was the only one for the last eight miles or so. He must have dozed for this last leg of the journey; although he had no memory of actually falling asleep he came to consciousness as the bus came into its destination. He peered from the window. His colleague had told him it was a market town but it looked no more than a village.

He alighted in a forlorn little market square with not a soul visible. He turned up his greatcoat collar against the wind and stamped up and down the wet cobblestones. The bus backed away, and settled, its engine turned off and its driver taking out a local newspaper and disappearing behind it. The few lamps shone, reflecting in the puddles. The western sky showed the vestiges of light through dark banked clouds. He felt cold and hungry. He awaited the sound of the car but there was nothing. He looked around, but there was no sign of a pub to shelter him, just a huddle of little grey houses, two shuttered shops and a bleak chapel, dead and uninviting. The sound of the bus engine startled him, its lights came back on, and it trundled away into the growing gloom. There was no sign of life.

He began to wonder if he'd been forgotten. What if no one came? He would have to knock on one of the blind darkened doors and ask for a bed for the night. The thought didn't hearten him much.

And then he heard the slow clip-clop of the horse's hoofs. He thought it would be a local farmer, but, as it rounded the corner, his astonishment rose. It was an old pony trap, the shrouded figure stared at him bringing the horse to a stop by where he stood. The driver said not a word.

'Are you from the Pingle?'

'Aye.' It was a thick accent.

The monosyllabic driver gave no sign he was going to assist with the luggage so Michael hoisted up the bags and climbed in. He noticed the curious emblem on the side, like a coat-of-arms in flecked gold print, but it wasn't a usual heraldic device. He couldn't make it out at first but then realised what it represented. It was a spider's web.

The driver touched the horse's back with his whip and it moved on again; turning, it headed out of the deserted market place.

The road wound on, between damp overhanging trees along the side of a valley. Michael tried conversation but there was no response. He buried himself deep within his coat and trusted that his host would be more communicative.

The miles seemed long and dreary through the darkening valley woods. Occasionally there was a farmhouse with a cluster of buildings and the rare lamp lit window behind shutters. He had never known such remoteness could lie in the British Isles. It was like a different, darkened, world.

After what seemed like hours of silence but for the plodding of the horse and the heavy drops of rain from the overhanging trees the driver turned the horse's head to the right through a great greystone arch, fortified like a castle. Michael noticed the blank eyes of empty windows to either side of what looked like deserted lodges and the strange motif emblazened in the stonework. A curious emblem like a spider's web.

The lane became narrowed and rutted, the trees closer still, dropping their heavy loads of rain water on the sides of the trap as it pushed past. He knew he was finally on Pingle land proper – though for many miles he knew he must be passing through the strange domain of this last absolute ruler in the land.

The land led upwards along the side of a narrow valley. A tumbling rushing torrent to their left and dark impenetrable trees shouldering each other to their right, dripping their wetness on his now sodden greatcoat.

The drive took him further and further into the tangled woodland. He couldn't calculate how far they were from the road. He had almost given up hope of seeing an end to the journey when suddenly the trees gave way to the thick dark foliage of rhododendron bushes, unruly and spreading across their path, and there, against the gloom, stood Llyspingle, enormous and dark. The foliage seemed to gather to its very walls. It was a great Gothic pile with arched windows and great studded door. Above the door incised in the granite was the emblem again: a spider's web.

The driver stopped the horse but gave no sign of helping him, so he got down taking his baggage. He thanked the driver who cracked his whip and the horse jolted on, along the drive which wound around the buttresses of the house – out of sight. He could hear its wheels squelching through the mud.

He turned to the door searching for a bell, a bell-pull at least he thought, but there was no need, the door was already open and a little woman in black smiled and silently bade him enter.

*

She took his coat and his two bags. The dark hall was warm; he noticed distinctly, how warm. There was no evidence of a fire, but from the damp cold outside suddenly coming into this ... The hall was large, its ceiling, far above, lost in the gloom, but that was not its main feature. The glass domes with stuffed creatures crowding it were what most caught his attention. He peered into them as he was led towards the stairs. There were all sorts of animals and birds. He was no expert in taxidermy but they struck him as not very good examples, contorted into strange shapes with their heads back and mouths open, their eyes wide with, he was not sure, could it be terror? And how emaciated they all looked, their hides drawn in as if the taxidermist had been short of stuffing. He smiled to himself. However peculiar the Pingle was he doubtless would not appreciate that observation.

They climbed the wide staircase, his hand resting a moment on the vast bannister; he withdrew it suddenly. The rail seemed coated in something soft, sticky, that pulled away with his withdrawn hand, sticky, like a web. He wiped it on his jacket extracting his fingers. It was a web, silken thread that pulled with him as he moved. He tugged his hand away and more of it moved, strands of it clinging to him, pulling other strands that hugged the bannister rail.

Suddenly a door opened at the stairhead. A figure stood there, tall and angular, with long thin arms. It darted back into the room, the door snapped shut.

The woman in front of him had stopped dead at the appearance. She had bowed her head and stooped slightly, almost like a curtsey. It was extraordinary. Michael moved past her, up the stairs, but the door was firmly closed. He turned to ask the question, but her face was impassive. She indicated to him to precede her and on they went, up the stairs along a corridor and up a further flight of steps, again the twisted animals. The warmth of the interior was making him perspire, not the healthy heat of a well ventilated building but an oppressive warmth, and damp. He could feel the perspiration beginning to trickle down his back.

She indicated a door and he opened it. The room was dark. He moved to enter and was arrested in his movement by a sound, a rustling scuttling sound; not like a mouse, he judged quickly, but about the same size, perhaps a little bigger – a dry rustling.

The woman had heard it too. She pushed past him into the darkness, gesticulating with her hands and pouring out a torrent of rapid Welsh, the first words he'd heard her speak. Light plays tricks with the eyes but he was almost sure he saw pinpricks of red light in clusters that darted about, disappearing from view. He had found the light switch and turned on a table lamp.

He looked around. The room was comfortable in a cluttered Victorian kind of way. He was relieved that there were no stuffed animals, but it was badly in need of a good dusting. Several of the corners and edges of the curtains were hung with what appeared to be cobwebs. He surreptitiously swept one down; but it clung to his hand – sticky and resilient – not at all like the dust of a cobweb.

The woman smiled at him, assuming a silent ignorance of what had just occurred, very much as she had done on the stairs. He was too polite to comment and he couldn't really complain at having mice in his room, or of the cobwebs. He was lucky to have been invited at all; but it did occur that someone as feudally powerful could be more concerned with the care of his house.

'Is the Pingle at home? Will I see him later?'

It was his first real attempt at conversation. The silence of his journey had let him grow accustomed to his own thoughts.

She smiled and nodded and in bad English indicated that he should come down to dinner when he was ready. She made her strange bow and left the room. He wondered if she usually spoke English. It was possible that Welsh was the major language this far west. He looked around, opening cupboard doors. Everything looked clean enough even if the corners of the rooms were rather cobwebby. He sorted out his clothes and washed. To his amazement the water in the jug was warm, as if the room had been just prepared for him. The bed seemed comfortable enough. The quilt already turned down, but he noticed a slight indentation on the pillow – as if something had rested there, it was too slight an indentation for someone's head. He put his hand upon the place, his fingers spread out, a slight indentation – about the size of a man's hand – spread out. He shivered suddenly with no reason the oppressive warmth reached even this far into the labyrinthine building; he was certainly not cold.

*

He found his way down to the hall again, more by luck than by judgement. He merely followed the law of the mountain walker following a stream; he took any direction downwards. The house was truly enormous with long darkened corridors leading this way and that, but he arrived in the hall as a clock somewhere was striking nine. Double doors to one side of the stairs stood open and he espied a long candlelit table. On entering he was met by a dark figure who turned upon him suddenly. He was tall and angular with what seemed a ridiculously small head set on his wide narrow shoulders. The pale face smiled at him, a joyless smile that didn't reach the dark set eyes. A long arm protruded towards him with a long fingered hand extended to shake his own. It was the Pingle.

'Mr Muffet, do forgive my rudeness in not welcoming you on your arrival.' The hand encased his; it was damp and clammy. The eyes searched his own.

'I'm afraid I was delayed … in the stables.'

It was a curious lie to begin a relationship. Michael knew it had been him who had appeared so suddenly at the stairhead, and then scuttled from view – but he made no mention of it.

'I'm so sorry you did not have more conversation in your journey.' The Pingle had read his mind, but what affected him most was the grip of the bony hand that still held his own. 'Alas few of my servants speak English – Welsh is the language here – and before I knew who had gone to collect you my foolish bailiff had sent someone who couldn't speak to you ... Would you like a drink?'

At last the grip was released and he could retrieve his crumpled hand. 'Yes, that would be splendid, thank you – a gin and tonic would be fine if you have one.'

The Pingle smiled his emotionless smile and stepped over to a sideboard. He had a distinctive way of moving; suddenly, with no warning he was gone to the sideboard clinking the glasses together.

'Ice?' He shot him a glance with the deep-set eyes.

'Thank you, yes.' And he was back, hunched over him, proffering the cut glass tumbler.

'To your work.' The Pingle touched his lips to the glass but Michael noticed he didn't drink.

'Come – sit down – you must be tired after your journey.' Again the rapid movement, over to a high-backed armchair on one side of a vastly empty fireplace. There was no need of a fire for the room was oppressively hot.

Michael was glad he had had the forethought to change into his lightest clothes.

'Tell me of your work. It seems most interesting – a study of feudal society, is it not?'

The meal progressed well enough. Michael was glad they sat at opposite ends of the table. For all his fastidiously quick movements the Pingle ate noisily, his mouth open when he chewed. It was a habit Michael could understand in a lonely bachelor, but it was one he always found somehow repellent. A number of servants waited at table coming and going in silence. It was almost as if the Pingle and he were the only two people present, so silent were the others.

He found it disquieting that his host seemed not to drink at all. His glass was filled and he raised it to his lips, but Michael noticed that he drank not a drop. Each glass for each course cleared away without comment or question by those who served them. The wine was very good, the food also. Conversation wandered on subjects as diverse as feudalism and the latest political news of the day. The Pingle certainly kept in touch with world events, although he explained that the mountains around made radio and television reception so poor as to eliminate the use of either. Telephones too were not used. There was no need when the whole of this little world was self-sufficient.

His particular pride was the electric generators that he had himself installed, driven by water power from the valley below the house. There was no need to rely on outside technology.

'But you must be tired.' The Pingle stood up suddenly, in the middle of what had seemed quite a successful conversation.

'Don't let me keep you from your sleep. There's time in the morning for me to show you around.'

Michael had the distinct feeling he was being dismissed. He looked at his watch. It was late, a little past midnight. He thanked his host who seemed almost to have forgotten his presence. They would meet in the morning.

There was no suggestion that he should be shown to his room so he left the dining room and wandered into the hall. The heat was the same here but he couldn't understand where it came from. He would ask in the morning if he wasn't too intimidated by his host.

He went up the stairs, but somehow wandered off his track a little, taking a wrong turning down a poorly lit passageway. He tried a number of doors but they were locked. The staring glass eyes of the stuffed animals didn't help his concentration, and the more doors he tried and the more he found locked the more disorientated he became. Quite suddenly, as if from nowhere, the tall shape of the Pingle was standing before him.

'My dear Mr Muffet, you're in quite the wrong direction – let me show you the way.'

A bony hand lay fleetingly on his shouler and he was led quickly away from the direction he had been taking, finding himself in a twinkling of an eye back at his own door.

His host opened the door for him and bade him sleep well. 'And if the heat troubles you do leave your windows open. The air is fresh up here.'

Michael found the light switch and turned to thank him but he found himself alone.

He entered the room again and prepared for sleep.

*

It was probably that the room was so hot or the bedclothes heavy upon him but he barely dozed; whenever he neared true sleep the recurring dream of his early childhood came back to haunt him, of spiders on his pillow. Half awake he would surely perceive one or two long legs feeling the air near his face, the sound of the rustling as the spider bodies climbed over one another. In his half slumber he turned the pillow, to cover the worrisome creatures, only to uncover a whole nest of brown crawling legs. He had nowhere but among them to lay his head. He reared up on his elbows to be away from the scuttering nest and awoke – it was a return to his childhood – leaning up in bed, the perspiration dripping from his face, his back quite damp.

He pummelled the pillow. Sure, even in the gloom, he saw something scuttle away, a dark shape the size of a man's outstretched hand, disappearing across the bed quilt and over the edge of the bed? He reached out for the light switch but it did not work, the generator was obviously turned off in the middle hours of the night.

Michael got out of bed and moved to the window gingerly pulling back the heavy curtains. Moonlight filled the room, falling across the bed. There was nothing there. He remained by the window. He hadn't followed the Pingle's suggestion of opening the casement. He should have done so earlier, he remembered. The Pingle had apologised for the heat, saying it was the necessity of an old man; he needed the warmth. He unfastened the latch and pushed at the window but there was a resistance. He looked out through the glass panes. There were strands of ivy or some creeper pressed against the window, two or three thick stems with no foliage. He pushed again at the window and there was a sudden noise. It startled him back into the room. A sudden angry hissing followed by a scampering noise like the sound of a rock climber descending a rock face, and a sharp clicking. The hissing receded rapidly away outside.

He returned to the window that had swung open with easy silence on well oiled hinges. He leant out looking to his left and right, puzzled. There was no sign of the creeper he had seen, there was nothing apart from a musty rather unpleasant smell, rather acrid. He looked far out to either side. The walls were sheer and clean of foliage. He was higher than he had imagined. A narrow terrace ran round the base of the wall and beyond its parapet another steep, dark drop. Obviously the house was built on the edge of a ravine. He could see the white tumbling water far below, and even hear its sound. But the walls were clear apart from a gathered shape far off to his right past the lower windows. Something clung there on the precipitous side of the old house like a gathered bunch of branches. It could be a large bush or small tree that had rooted in the stonework.

He edged back, leaning his elbows on the window ledge breathing in the air; the acrid smell had gone, and now it was good clean air, damp but clear after the rain. He stayed thus for some minutes – until a movement called his attention. Something brushed past him, climbing up beside him and scuttling away down the wall.

He recoiled against the window. It had been an enormous spider. It stopped some yards below him, bunching its legs. It was the size of a man's outstretched hand. He had never seen any spider so large – he was riveted to the spot, watching it in fascination. Somehow he wasn't frightened. It amazed him that he wasn't, but somehow the calculating analytical part of his brain had taken over; for the first time he felt free of his secret fear.

It must have crept up the curtain at his side when he was craning out of the window. He could see its red pinpricks of eyes in the dark and then it turned scuttling down the wall. He was too fascinated to withdraw.

It moved away to the right down past the next row of darkened windows. Suddenly there was flurry of movement, the mass of tangled branches suddenly moved and with a lightning movement the spider was engulfed and a piercing scream met his ears. The spider had disappeared from view. He watched on and on and he thought he detected a small movement amongst those tangled branches but nothing more. For the first time in the house he felt suddenly cold. He realised how vulnerable he was standing by the window amongst the curtains. His analytical detachment began to recede. He recalled other pinpricks of red light that he had first seen in the room. He listened for movement in the darkened bedroom. He was aware of the webs that clung to the corners of the curtains.

He crossed the room gingerly, seeking the candle that stood by the door he found it – his hearing acute – and strained as he fumbled for the matches; he was sure he could hear the rustling of movement by the still open window.

The match flared to life bringing sudden yellow light to the room. His eyes were caught by what lay over the window ledge; long and stretched out, it searched fastidiously, feeling its way through the opening that he had left for it. What he had taken as creeper pressed against the glass, what he had taken as a bunch of branches clinging to the wall was a single gigantic spider's leg matted with brown hair. The tip of another appeared on the window-sill easing its way into the room. He fled, unfastening the door; he fled, shielding the candle from his headlong flight down the corridor and the steps – and he didn't know which way to run. But he fled, past the contorted animals he had thought the work of an amateur taxidermist, past their terror-stricken eyes and gaping mouths and the bodies emaciated and sapped of life. The shadows danced and weaved in his barefoot passing. He had left the door open. He realised that the bedroom door allowed the creature into the house. He ran on, his breath catching, his chest heaving. His headlong flight slowed. He didn't know which way he had come, but he recognised some of the furnishings. He rested,

leaning against a door frame. It had been here that he had met
the Pingle. Perhaps he was in one of the rooms. Michael
looked about, if he could get to the Pingle, to tell
him ...

He tried a door handle and it gave, it swung open; steps led
downwards. The candlelight didn't give much visibility, but he
stepped down. The room echoed. It could be another way to
the hall. Following the notion that down must lead to the hall,
he descended, but as he stepped further he noticed the feeling
of threads upon his bare feet, the soft pull of web at his elbow.
He looked about holding the candle higher.

The whole chamber was festooned with white web. He
stood stock still, his eyes searching in fear for movement but
there was none. He was alone. The chamber was cavernous.
Thick white web hung from ceiling to floor, some thicker than
elsewhere had openings, like wide tunnels.

He could see a door below him, and edged towards it. Here
and there objects hung from the thicker areas of web like large
chrysalises, dark and dead. He paused by one which hung close
to the stair. Holding his candle high he became aware of what
it was. Disfigured and crumpled to less than its full stature it
hung, a fragile empty shape, elbows sticking out at distorted
angles, its head drawn down to its chest; hollow and paper thin,
it was the remains of a man.

He cast a wandering eye over the other objects that hung in
the gloom of the web, the empty husks of former trophies,
each one now detectable as the remains of humans – like
himself. He moved hesitatingly towards the door his mind still
working, miraculously still functioning. The creature he had
seen – the creature of this lair – was a pet. It must be some
incredible macabre pet of the Pingle. He was an arachnidologist; he must have bred the monstrous thing; he must
know about these ... people. He gained the door at the bottom
of the stairs. He tried the handle – it turned – and he
blundered through the door slamming it shut behind
him.

He stood looking around, the candle flickered and

spluttered. He was on the main stairs, the stairs that led down
to the hall, he had come up them earlier that same evening. He
turned to look at the door. The web trailed out from under it.
He could see it glistening on the bannister rail. It had been this
same door at which he first caught sight of the Pingle on his
way up the stairs. His hand had delved into some of the web,
had pulled at it, like a fly caught – and the door had flown
open and the Pingle himself had stood there, for a few
moments, before retreating again; retreating into his pet's lair.

*

He stood against the panelled wall incapable of further
movement, incapable of decision-making. His mind – now
out of immediate danger – had stopped its frantic
working.

A door opened below, the dining room door, flooding the
hall with light. The tall figure of his host emerged and looked
up.

'Why – Mr Muffet – whatever are you doing there?'

His host sounded concerned, civil, ordinary. Michael
remained transfixed unable to move.

The Pingle turned on the electric light. The several lamps on
the stairs lit up. It was ordinary, normal. His host came up the
stairs towards him, his face concerned.

'I know I keep late hours, but, my dear Mr Muffet, what is
wrong?'

Michael managed to stammer an apology, his thoughts still
in the chamber behind the door with its gruesome trophies.

The man was beside him, looking down at him from his
considerable height.

'Do come down. You look unwell. May I get you a drink – a
brandy perhaps?'

He led him down the steps away from the door, a gentle but
firm grip on his pyjama-clad form.

The transformation from nightmare to reality was too
difficult. He accepted the large brandy and willingly drank

deep. The Pingle sat opposite him looking intent.

'It was a nightmare, I expect ... the journey ... perhaps even the heavy meal. I hope not the cooking?'

The attempt at humour from the humourless smiling face was difficult to assimilate.

Michael didn't know what to do. This urbane and civil man must know what lay beyond the door. He couldn't be oblivious to the things Michael had himself just witnessed ... or could he? Was it all his own imaginings? Certainly the Pingle was odd, but what he envisaged was too monstrous.

'Have another drink? You look as if you need one. My dear fellow, I feel responsible. What a thing to happen to a guest on his first night.'

He handed the glass back. It was very full. Michael began to regain some notion of normality. It was as if he had returned to childhood, sitting by the drawing room fire trying to explain his nightmare to his parents, but still having it cling to him – still partly asleep ... He had had a lot of nightmares as a child and always spiders. It was called arachnoiphobia. He had even seen a specialist about it, but the man had said he would grow out of it. He drank deep of the brandy ... it warmed him. The specialist had been not unlike the Pingle, sitting there as he did now, the reflection of the firelight making his eyes look red ... But there wasn't a fire. His host moved one of his arms but another seemed to protrude from his back, over the back of the chair. The drink was blurring his sight. The Pingle looked as if he had more than two eyes, more than four ... and his legs were longer surely, and thinner ... and his movements more jerky ... as he bunched himself ... for a final jump ...

*

Michael awoke with a start. His head had hit the window of the bus. He looked around wide-eyed, his heart beating quickly ... It took some moments to realise where he was; the bus – the journey. The other passengers had alighted. He was alone. It was getting dark outside and beginning to rain as the bus trundled on through the lanes. His greatcoat around him – his two cases on the rack above his head. He was on the bus. He had fallen asleep. The journey had taken so long. His heart was still beating at a feverish rate, the fear still upon him – it took time for it to subside and the incredible relief began to flow, the realisation that it had been a dream, the most terrible of all his dreams. He looked at his watch. Nearly seven o'clock. He must have slept for an hour, but the relief! He could cry out with the relief. He wouldn't of course; he had to look out at the countryside and breathe deeply. Never had he had such a terrible vivid dream, but he wouldn't think of it … the fear had lain buried for so long he had never thought it would erupt again, and with such terror! He tried to settle himself, his heart had slowed to nearer its normal rate. He felt dry-mouthed. He looked at his watch again. He would be arriving soon.

He looked out of the window, the first few houses began to show. It didn't look a particularly big place. His colleague had said it was a market town …

The bus rattled to a halt and he gathered his things together and got down. It was a forlorn little market square with not a soul visible. He had expected a car to be waiting for him but there was no one about. Even the houses looked dark and deserted.

The coach backed into a corner of the square, the engine was turned off and the driver began to read a newspaper. Michael turned his collar up and began to walk up and down the wet cobbles. He had a strange feeling as if he'd been to this place before, but the thoughts of the terror of his dream still reared and he tried to push them away.

He looked for a pub to shelter him while he waited but there wasn't one, just a couple of shuttered `shops and a grim-looking chapel.

The coach engine started again. Its lights came on and he watched it trundle away.

He was beginning to think he'd been forgotten when he heard the steady clip-clop of a horse's hoofs.

A pony and trap came in sight with a driver muffled against the cold ...

Little Miss Muffet
Sat on a tuffet
Eating her curds and whey;
There came a big spider
Who sat down beside her

V

House Spirit

In the dark, dark wood there is a house ...

It was the end of the summer term that the boys were told, the
Housemaster had left it to the last minute, he knew what their
reaction would be. They hated change in the school ... he
summoned up his courage.

The dining hall was hot, even with the windows open, the
white sunlight had drained the colour from the fields, a warm
breeze shifted the curtains, high summer. They sat before him
– waiting.

'... to become truly co-educational. It has been decided to
follow the example of some other schools ... and introduce
mixed houses ... six girls will be arriving in this house next
term – they will be the first group.'

He lifted his chin, swallowing – he could feel a trickle of
perspiration beginning to run down his temple.

'Are there any questions?'

There was a hush, the junior boys were the only ones to look
pleased. Heavy silence held the assembly in its grip. Davis, the
Head of House, moved uncomfortably, examining his fingers
– he had been told a week ago – and the night before had
spoken to the House Sixth.

They sat in a brooding silence. He could feel their eyes upon
him. They had delegated him to ask the question, he coughed,
and raised his eyes to meet the housemaster's defensive glare.

'We wondered ... Sir ... we were wondering about ... House
Spirit ... Sir ... it will be different ... difficult.'

'Difficult!' The Housemaster's voice was harsh, betraying
tension, but he moderated:

'... the Spirit of the House as you call it, Davis, is something that has absorbed many changes; it is not a static thing, you know ... it is not ...' He searched for a word. 'It is not some kind of mysogynistic entity in the building. The Spirit of the House is made up of the people in it – whether they be boys or girls – it makes no difference ... There have been many changes before, many things have been absorbed into the Spirit of the House.'

He was sounding reasonable, but they sat implacably, unyielding to his entreaties.

'Take the abandoning of fagging, for example. We have to move with the times.'

There was a murmur of disapproval. Of all the senior boys, only Peterson – the ladykiller – was enthusiastic.

'Where will they sleep, sir?'

The Housemaster eyed Peterson – he knew well the boy's reputation, and had his answer ready. It had been a brilliant piece of outmanoeuvre, he thought, to put them in that particular room, in that particular part of the house. Schoolboys were unerringly traditional, clinging to the most foolish of outmoded ideas. The use of that one room would put the rest off, and even slow Peterson down. It had been curiously taboo for as long as the housemaster could remember – some stupid schoolboy folkmyth of evil long ago ... It had been locked and barred when he had become Housemaster, and no one could tell him why, but the turmoil among the boys when the room was opened was amazing. He had wanted to use it as a common room, but none of the boys would go in it.

'They will have the east rooms as their study block, and their dormitory will be the Gaff.'

There was an almost audible gasp from the assembled boys. Even the Head of House hadn't known that.

'But, sir ... you can't!'

'Oh, but Davis, I have ... I don't know how you can countenance all this nonsense, about that room being haunted.

I can assure you that girls won't be so scared about things as you seem to be.'

'But the stories of boys disappearing from that room ... that séance in the east rooms years back ... with the six faces appearing in the wall.'

'You see, gentlemen ... you wouldn't use the rooms yourselves, so why shouldn't we house the girls there? You won't even go into the east rooms to store your trunks – it is always Matron who has to go. They make the ideal set of rooms – and at the moment they're just full of junk, the Gaff itself has been locked and empty for years. It is a waste of space. It will be redecorated during the summer holidays.'

The boys left the meeting in a subdued mood, whilst a few of the hardier ones went up to explore.

The house in its upper reaches was rambling and ancient – the oldest part of the school buildings. Thick walls and small arched windows – winding passageways, a labyrinth. It had never been part of any restoration work and was probably the only original building left.

Masters, the second prefect, approached the ancient studded door. Davis held back a little, he had always found it strangely cold up here. He looked around.

'This must be almost the dead centre of the school.'

'Oh, very drôle, Davis – the dead centre.'

'Well, it's as cold as a tomb, and dark – have you noticed ... it's blazing hot out there, but up here it's really cold.' He shivered.

'Well, the girls might warm it up!'

Peterson grinned as he peered out of one of the small windows.

'This must be the old tower.' He looked back into the passageway.

'You wouldn't notice it from the inside, but do you remember Davis climbing on the roofs the term before last? This bit is away from the rest, sticking up ... that's why it's cold. You see, no spooky cold, they are all outside walls.'

Master looked up from examining the door.

'That would make a lot of sense, Peterson, if it weren't so hot outside ...'

He looked at Davis.

'Physics was never one of his strong points.'

He turned back to the door.

Peterson was unabashed – looking around, he began to hum a tune to himself.

Masters looked up. 'Have you ever noticed this? It's covered with something.'

Davis stepped forward to study it. Masters traced his fingers over the surface.

'You see, around the nailheads, it's like ... like leather.'

Davis scrutinized it.

'Yes, – it must have been covered once – but it's all coming away.'

He put out his hand and touched the surface; a large piece flaked off, coming away. He examined it closely, it began to break up, dusty in his hand.

'It's too lightweight for leather,' he pondered. 'It looks like ...'

Peterson arrested his attention, clutching at his arm, he pointed. The black ring handle of the door had begun to move, very slightly, silently, it had begun to turn. They had not touched it – it was being turned from the inside ... the door was being opened from the inside.

They didn't wait to see, they knew everyone else was out of this part of the building. And the Housemaster himself had said the room was locked and empty – no one ever came here. They left the place. The piece of dried covering from the door lay crumbled on the floor outside the room.

They did not speak of the incident to anyone – it had been an undignified rush through that winding dark labyrinth; they had arrived breathless in the light and warmth at the bottom of the stairs. Peterson had vowed at that moment not to trouble the girls who were coming, they were welcome to their quarters, he would be glad to get away for the holidays.

*

There had been a number of difficulties in getting the girls' quarters ready, and the Housemaster was heartily sick of the business by the end of the holidays. Problems of power cables not working, the workmen complaining of the cold in the area, particularly in the Gaff itself. He had enquired if it was absolutely necessary for several men to be working together in the room, when there were other places that needed attention. But the foreman said that they had refused to work there alone. It left the Housemaster infuriated.

The decorators had great trouble with the walls of the room; they found it very difficult to clean them, saying that whatever had been used to paint it originally was terribly difficult to get off. It seemed to have impregnated the plaster through to the stones of the walls themselves, a faded red colour, with a texture like matted hair.

Several discoveries were made, too. A tin box with papers in it, and around the edges of the skirting board, some granulated white dust. The workmen removed a quantity before they could get the electric wiring finished. And then the other discovery – something else, rather unpleasant – teeth, buried in the gap between the skirting and the floor boards. The Housemaster took samples of both finds to the science department for examination.

The Biology Master said the teeth were certainly human, probably those of a young person, and the powder – calcium – he guessed was powdered bone of some kind. He asked where the finds had been made. But the Housemaster was unenthusiastic to explain, merely saying they had been found whilst digging – they were apparently quite old. The Housemaster was secretly perturbed by these rather gruesome finds, and he wondered if there could be some grain of truth in the traditions about evil in the room.

He spent some evenings examining the contents of the tin box, which appeared to be the private papers of a predecessor who had been Housemaster in the 1780s. He scanned the journals for anything pertaining to the sinister which could explain the discoveries in the room.

There were several recorded incidents of death among the pupils from various diseases; these of course were quite common in those days. There were records of how sports were played, and a record of matches, but as his tenure of office went on, other entries began to appear; odd episodes regarding the disappearance of boys from what was described as 'The Tower Room'. The Housemaster thought about the room, but it would be impossible to find out where the particular room was now – such had been the architectural rearrangements of the school. In fact, he paused to remember – somewhere he had heard of nineteenth-century plans for the tower to be dismantled – and the stone used for a new cemetery on the edge of town. A curious story. Funny things the Victorians got up to – but that was probably what happened.

He returned to the journal. The entries of the disappearances were scrawled in a spidery hand in a curious dull red ink. The first few only noted the disappearances, but the last entries were fuller.

The fifth boy has disappeared – but no great comment – the guardians are not interested in a search, they believe he has run away as he did before, and I have encouraged their belief ... it is good to choose the ones with no family – they are the best ... only two more now ...

And later, some notes written in the same red ink, with passion – even now so long after, he could see how the pen had dug into the page.

The school is being changed around me, these new ideas disgust me, I hate change, the ways of our ancient knowledge are trampled by the ignorance of modern thought. I am the Alpha and Omega, not their petty Christian beliefs. These buildings have become part of me. I part of them, how dare they ... I was here before they existed and will remain into years yet unknown. My spirit freed will reign throughout the ages. They whisper against me, these little men – I know they plot – they speak of alchemy – the fools – if only they knew the truth.

And later, another entry of similar type …

The sixth boy has been delivered to the room … he made no trouble for me … only one more, and I will be free of this curse of flesh – my spirit will be free to live as long as stone stands on stone. It is the ancient remedy to absorb seven young souls for perpetual life. The next on 'All Hallows' Eve' – it is appropriate.

But there, the entries stopped.

The Housemaster searched through empty pages, but whatever had been planned for 'All Hallows' Eve' had not been recorded, or had not happened – yet. He stopped himself. What an odd thing to think – 'Yet' … he discarded it. But he had been intrigued enough to follow up his investigation in the official school records. He found only scant reference to the distant predecessor, but it made interesting reading.

The new Headmaster, Dr Godfrey, had found some of the traditions of the school to be inappropriate to his more modern thoughts upon the Christian education of young people, and clashed a number of times with the senior housemaster, Dr H. H. Mulleneux. In his explanation of Dr Mulleneux's dismissal, the Headmaster said.

'The Reverend Doctor was found to be unsuitable for his work in this establishment, and has been dismissed. There has been mounting evidence for his involvement in the ancient Italian blasphemy of …

Then the account had been scratched out.

At the end of the erased section, he noticed the words – 'and it has been shuttered and barred from further use as the spirits of evil live long in the stones.' And a biblical reference

'Leviticus 14.43-48.' He didn't bother to look it up; it was all so long ago, and he had wasted enough time on it anyway.

The room was redecorated in a brighter decor and the curious strips of what looked like leather that he had noticed were removed from the door. The door looked much better cleaned, but he noticed the initials deep carved in the lintel 'H.H.M. Alpha and Omega', and then an inscription:

Lasciate Ogni Speranza Voi Che Entrate.

He thought he would have the inscription plastered over – one of the girls might be a Dante enthusiast. It was lucky none of the workmen could read Italian. It was obviously all some foolish superstition. Best to ignore it.

The girls arrived early to get settled in, and when they were taken up into the east rooms, the Housemaster and his wife were pleased with their reactions. The effect of carpeting and new lamps was good and the six girls chatted happily at they were shown around. The difficult moment arose when they found the door of the Gaff jammed, but after a few hefty pushes by the Housemaster, it opened easily.

The girls seemed suddenly silent when they entered the room, but the Housemaster and his wife gave them cheery instructions and were both pleased by the general effect of the new duvets and curtaining. Even the tell-tale marks of the crowbars on the skirting board had been covered by the thick pile carpet, and the inscription over the door had been covered up. They left the girls in the room to get used to it, and told them that tea would be ready in half an hour. As they walked away the door of the room slammed shut – they looked at one another, hoping that they hadn't made a mistake – hoping that one of the girls wasn't going to be petulant and difficult. The prospect of girls slamming doors was not really to their liking.

*

Curiously, it was the same idea that taxed the girls' minds – to have the door slammed on them like that seemed a little aggressive of the Housemaster and his wife. It seemed a little too like a prison. The room itself they felt wore a strange air, as if somehow, something lurked there – waiting. They didn't altogether like it.

As the days went on, they developed a series of routines to cope with their feelings about the room. Whenever they returned after house supper, they made sure not to be alone. They always left the light on when they went out in the evening so that the room was never in darkness, and they always tried to leave the door open. But somehow it was always closed when they returned, and the light would be off. They blamed each other for this at first, or wondered whether the boys were playing tricks on them. But the boys, by some common consent, seemed never to venture near the room, and would not speak of it to the girls.

On occasions of returning along those passageways and opening the door on that empty dark room, the girls received the strangest impression. They all confessed to have felt it ... Somehow as if they had disturbed something, as if in their absence something had been happening there, that they didn't know about ... and that, as the certainty began to grow upon them, they didn't want to know.

It was chance, perhaps, that that year the autumn exeat ended on 31st October. They had all decided to meet in London and make the journey back to school together, but Clare lived nearer than the rest, and when her guardian was told of the rail strike that had trapped the other girls in London, he drove Clare to school.

The Housemaster and her guardian together assured her that nothing could possibly happen to her, left alone for one night. The others would be arriving during the next afternoon. It was her guardian, particularly, who grew angry at her insistence that she didn't want to sleep in the dormitory on her own. The boys had something of a Hallowe'en party, which went well, and the house was quiet at 11.30.

The Housemaster's wife had a disturbed night, waking several times to say that she heard screaming – but all was quiet

– she went back to sleep. Then awakening again to say she had such terrible, realistic dreams, of a darkness and terrifying panic of not being able to escape – she said she couldn't open the door – but which door she couldn't describe. And then she said that it was at her back – tearing at her flesh, actually tearing it off. But the Housemaster pacified her, and said it was the Hallowe'en party punch, and he wouldn't make it so strong next year. They slept again.

November 1st dawned with an unusual occurrence – Clare had not come down to breakfast – and the Head of House was sent to knock on the door.

He returned saying there was no answer – but to his friends he observed that the door had changed, it had been re-covered. Masters had been right, he said, it wasn't leather, it was skin that was stretched and nailed to the door. He had noticed something else as well; some plaster had come off the door lintel and there was an inscription in Italian – it was a quote from Dante, 'Abandon Hope all Ye who enter here.'

Davis was in the study when the Housemaster returned from forcing the door to the room; the Housemaster looked shaken, he said – pale. He told the other senior boys about it as they stood by the window watching the arrival of the school doctor and the Chaplain.

'It was odd … I don't know what could have happened … he was muttering something about the walls … he said "It wasn't paint" … and something about powder in the corners of the room …'

Peterson stared out of the window.

'He's flipped – lost his marbles – I expect she's only run away or something. She did from her last school, or so she told me.'

'No … I'm sure there's more to it than that … He was really shaken up … Before he sent me out he said something about someone called Mulleneux having taken her … something about it all matching up and her having a guardian and no family, and something about her being the seventh and it being All Hallows' Eve. He was very confused – it didn't make sense at all – any of it. Oh yes, and some rubbish about me being right, about the Spirit of the House ... but it hadn't been me that said it, it was him ... last term.'

'What do you mean?'

'Well, it was him, wasn't it ... that said the Spirit of the House would absorb the girls.?'

In the dark dark wood there is a house
In the dark dark house there is a room
In the dark dark room there is ...

VI

The Ship in a Bottle

Bobby Shafto's gone to sea ...

The room was perfect with old beams and deep set windows, but the view gave it that special quality: the harbour, the fishing boat lights coming on as dusk settled, and the sound that accompanied the view and the sea washing against the stone harbour wall coming up to them through the warm evening air.

It was still light enough to make out the headland, purple against the darkening sapphire of the ocean beyond.

James put the case down.

'Like it?'

'It's beautiful, beautiful.'

Sarah smiled at him, taking his hand. 'It's so perfect.'

She came into his arms – a soft embrace.

'Well, this is Cornwall.' He spoke into her corn-coloured hair, her soft cheek against his.

'It's been worth the journey – I'm glad we didn't stay over at the hotel.'

James was glad too. The wedding had been marvellous, of course, and the reception great fun – but to escape to the sea, that was a truly perfect end to the day. Even the best of people could be too much after a while and the long journey had been a good excuse not to overstay at the reception.

He looked out past her hair to the view. With her in his arms and the sea in his view he had everything he could want.

There was a permanence in having someone who loved one, someone to wait for him, someone to come back home to. He knew she didn't want him to go to sea, but it had been his first love. He had explained that, she knew it, and when his permanent commission had come through – only three weeks ago though it seemed far longer – she had gone through with the wedding. He had really thought she wouldn't, but she had and now he had them both.

Her embrace became tighter. She moved her head and looked into his eyes.

'You don't want to go out, do you?' He had wanted to go down to the harbour to show her the ships, but she held him, moving him a little from the window.

'We can go out tomorrow, can't we? You don't want to go out now, do you?' She led him gently towards the bed.

*

The bright sunshine lit the waves, sparkling. The gulls screeched over the fishing boats as they unloaded the night's catch. She held his hand. She looked so beautiful in her light flowing frock.

'It's a marvellous place.' Her gaze took in the tumbling houses that piled upon each other above the harbour and the whirling white of the gulls against the blue.

'These streets are intriguing.' She led him away from the boats, to explore the cobbled lanes that rose steeply into the dark recesses of the town.

He followed, happy with her enthusiasm. He hadn't known the town well. A friend had told him of the hotel and he wanted to share the exploring with her. A corner of his county he hadn't known before; to share it now was good.

She led the way, holding his hand, up the winding lane between the close packed whitewashed houses, lane leading on to lane, cobbled alleyways, nooks and corners.

It was she who first saw the little shop, hardly visible in a shuttered corner. The window, though, once spied had an inviting quality; small panes, stacked with the oddments of a maritime past, old telescopes, swords and tackle, higgledy-piggledy, dusty, forgotten. The gold figured name over the doorway was flaked away. She peered in through the window, cupping her hands against the glass, shielding her view from the bright sunlight.

'Do let's go in – it's a *real* junk shop.'

And it was, the real thing, high up in a forgotten back lane, untrammelled by the tourist trade; it was a forgotten jewel.

They picked through oddments, brass and mahogany, enjoying the quiet mustiness a good ten minutes before the elderly proprietor made his appearance, a grey-whiskered old man in faded jersey and baggy trousers, a real old sailor – he even had a hook instead of a left hand.

'Lookin' for anythin' particular, my dears?'

Sarah was bright – a thing out of place in the dinginess.

'No, not really. I want a wedding present for my husband.' She held out her hand and took James's. He was a little embarrassed. It wasn't really the thing to tell a stranger.

The old man only smiled though and picked through his things lovingly. He seemed to know them all as if they were friends.

'Not many folks come up here – we must try to find something special.'

James looked about along the crowded shelves of books and cutlasses, old bottles and faded cobwebbed model boats. The old man looked too, immediately, to a place high up. James followed his gaze.

His attention settled on the thing at the same instant as Sarah's, high up on its shelf. But he could see immediately that it was a fine example. She saw it too and knew instinctively. She smiled at him and then at the old man.

'Could we have a look at that?' It would be expensive; even without tourist trade prices it was bound to be expensive ...

'Ah yes, my prized possession. You've a good eye, that's for sure. It's the very thing you've come for.'

James cursed her enthusiasm; that certainly wouldn't be the way to get a bargain. He wondered how often things were called 'prized possessions' by shopkeepers about to make a sale.

The old man carefully unfolded some steps and made his way wheezingly to the top shelf. He dusted the bottle with his hand –

almost as if he were caressing it – and brought it down, gingerly. The bottle was old, James could see that at a glance, but the model itself was beautifully intricate, each spar and fine pale line of rigging a masterpiece of care. He didn't really mind the idea of price once he had scrutinised the interior of the bottle. It was a museum piece. The model itself certainly looked contemporary with the age of the sloop of war it was made to resemble, late eighteenth-century. He felt he must possess it even if it were terribly expensive.

He hadn't realised just how intently he had been gazing at it until his attention was drawn from the article to the other two people in the small room, watching him.

'Yes, it's a fine piece that's for sure.' The old man looked down at it, no sign of deceit in his face. He was simply sharing the admiration.

James picked it up and they all studied it in silence.

The tiny intricate details of the deck furnishings, the incredibly fine ropework and painting.

When Sarah finally broke the silence, it was with something of a hush in her voice.

'It must have taken months and months –'

'Of loving care,' the old man added. James looked up from examining the name inscribed on the stern of the ship.

'Do you know its history then?' The old man had appeared to speak from knowledge. But he just smiled a whiskery smile.

'Not really, my dear – just a surmise on my part.'

James looked into the clear blue eyes of the old face. It was curious … the first time he had felt there to be a trace of untruth in what the old man said. For a moment he detected something of the closed quality of the professional antique dealer. He felt a little disappointed; he had warmed to the genuineness of this old sailor. But it was only a hint, and it wasn't something to affect the price.

Sarah had picked the bottle up. It was the first time she had held it. James didn't notice at first; he was absorbed in the problem of how to approach the question of the price.

'My love he wants to go to sea …'

It was a curious thing to tell the old man – but the tone was the thing that recalled his thoughts.

'I don't want him to go; to leave me for the sea ...' That really was too much. James came back from his calculations. The old man was staring at her and Sarah, who had been gay and carefree, stood stock still, the bottle held in her two hands; her eyes stared straight ahead without seeing, trance-like.

'I will hold his hand, hold his hand and he will be forever mine ...'

James looked at her; he couldn't understand what was going on, but the old man's reaction was extraordinary. He gently took the bottle from her, taking it carefully from her fingers, and gently, very gently, said to her:

'You daren't let him go then, my dear, don't you fear now. It'll all come right for 'e, I'm only here to help you now ... and you too can help me in this. 'Twas meant that you should take it for me.' There was no surprise in his lilting Cornish voice, like some old country doctor rather than a little old fellow in a tiny forgotten junk shop. But it was an odd thing for him to say to her – it would have seemed impertinent in another context, but so quickly was the exchange of words completed that James had no time to object.

Immediately the old man had taken it from her grasp Sarah was again herself, showing interest in the detail of the ship, giving no hint that anything odd had happened. The old man too seemed to ignore the incident. Before James could comment they were deep in conversation about how ships were got into bottles, the old man holding it up and pointing out how the masts could be folded flat; the only indication of what had just passed lay, James noticed, in the fact that the old man didn't give it to Sarah to hold and, although they were discussing it in detail, neither did she appear to want to hold it.

It was as if the incident hadn't happened. And so convincing were the two that James felt curiously as if it had been he alone who had witnessed the occurrence. He recalled himself to his senses, interrupting their discussion:

'We ought to be thinking about a price ...' The old man looked up.

'Oh yes ...' He placed the bottle on a nearby counter and pulled at his whiskers with his one hand, eyeing the model, and then looking up at Sarah who, James noticed, gazed at the bottle fixedly.

'Is it not for a wedding present?' Sarah looked up, bright.

'Yes, my husband always liked these sorts of things – he has just received his commission to go to sea as a ship's medical officer.'

Again it was unnecessary to tell him, but this time in her own voice. The old man smiled.

'And so it should be I who should be discussing it with the lady, sir.'

James should have felt irritated as he was hustled out of the shop, but the old man and she were so conspiratorial it would have been silly to protest.

He felt in his jacket pocket and realised that he had their new shared cheque book; she really couldn't spend that much on it if it was for cash.

He awaited her arrival in the sunlight. He really didn't know how he was going to find their way back to the hotel; this part of the town was a maze of winding, whitewashed houses crowded together, almost meeting across the narrow passageways that burrowed between them.

The shop door opened and out emerged Sarah followed by the old man holding a brown paper parcel. He gave it into James's hands. James was reminded of the times as a junior houseman he had seen nurses carrying babies out of the hospital not allowing the mother to hold it, but safely delivering them off the premises. It was a funny thing to recall.

'I hope you will both be happy together – may you be together a long time.'

It was a nice thing for him to say, and Sarah thanked him again and then James did, and he watched them down the narrow cobbled lane. They turned at the end of the lane to look back, and there he was, still watching them, a gentle benign smile on his whiskered face. And then they turned a corner and saw him no more.

'How much was it?'

'I'm not allowed to say,' she smiled at him.

'About how much?'

She looked at him, the smile playing about her mouth.

'Believe it or not he tried to give it to me – to make our marriage complete, he said. But I wasn't having that so I forced some money on him, it wasn't much.'

'How incredible.'

'Wasn't it? But he was so kind. He said it cheered his heart to see us and he'd give the money to some fund they've got for seafarers or something.'

'I must take you antique hunting more often – you've got the knack!'

'And you've got the present.'

He looked at the parcel in his hands.

'Thank you, darling – it's just what I would have wanted.'

'I know,' she said and linked her arm through his, leaning her head on his shoulder as they made their way down the winding alleyways in the sunshine.

*

At first James blamed the shell-fish they had had for supper. They had gone to bed quite early – it was after all only the second night of their honeymoon – but he was awoken by her thrashing about and crying out, a strange gasping cry as if in anguish. The moon was up and shining full and clear across the harbour and through the windows. It illuminated the ship in the bottle by the bedside. As he struggled vainly to awaken her his eyes took in the model by her side. There was a curious sensation, as if the ship were moving in its bottle. As her cries became more frantic so too the movements of the ship, as if tossed by monstrous waves heeling over as if it would capsize and all hands be lost. He could almost hear the crew calling out across the waves, the gasping cries of Sarah mingling with them, making him turn the more frantic in his attempts to rouse her.

She came gasping to consciousness with a name on her lips.

'Bobby ... Bobby,' and fell into his arms sobbing, damp, as if with perspiration, but he felt too damp for that. An odd notion struck him, that she too had witnessed the loss of the ship on the shore and had run desperate and unheeding into the breakers.

They slept after that and the following day blamed the lobster. But she was silent during the morning and he caught her looking at him at times with a strange expression as if she would say something but she didn't dare. They had meant to go swimming that day but by unspoken agreement they drove inland to safer sites of the old tin mines, away from the breakers that creamed onto the rocks along the coast.

*

They had been in bed some time. She held him to her, an almost desperately tight grip.

'You wouldn't think of going into general practice, would you?'

He pulled her away, holding her by her shoulders and looking into her eyes. Hers searched his, with that particular look of apprehension and guilt. They had discussed this before.

'You know we've talked this out. We have agreed.'

He shook her shoulders gently.

'We agreed.' He repeated it. He loved her so much, but he repeated it. She had known before their wedding he was destined for the sea.

'Last night I had this terrible dream. You were on board a ship but it was sinking, in terrible seas. I was so frightened.'

He held her to him stroking her hair.

She spoke to his chest.

'The breakers were coming right over it. I saw the masts give way – you were hanging on the rigging.'

He could see the ship in its bottle beyond her, the fine rigging and masts so intricately made ... and he could see the picture she painted with her words. He had seen the loss of that ship himself.

'It was only a dream – you know it was, the excitement.' He moved her away – holding her at arm's length, and smiled.

'It was the lobster!'

That night there was no recurrence; which gave weight to the lobster argument. But still the next morning she wore the slightly distanced look of someone who desperately wanted her own way, but wouldn't be open about it. They spent the day on the beach.

It flitted through his mind more than once that she was using the nightmare as a tool to get her own way. He hardened his attitude when that thought occurred, and he would not notice her silence.

They had already agreed; there was no argument. He would take up his commission and he would go to sea. It niggled at him that she had now married him and was attempting to change the rules they had laid down. It simply wasn't on, and if necessary she would have to lump it. But the thought made him unhappy.

That night the wind had risen and rain spattered heavily on the window panes. As they lay in bed they could hear thunder muttering further down the county. The hotelier had told them that it would probably blow itself out by morning, so they snuggled warm together under the covers of their bed. She slept first and James drifted slowly, contentedly, into sleep as the storm rolled nearer.

He was startled awake, probably by the simultaneous flash and earth-searing crash of the storm overhead. But in the instant he was awake and in the weird white blaze of the lightning that illuminated the room knew that she was gone – and with her, the ship in its bottle.

The bed was rumpled and cold, the door onto the landing open. By the next lightning flash that followed on the heels of the rolling thunder he was out, his dressing gown already round him. By intuition he followed – no turning aside, he knew. Down the stairs, the front door too, unbolted and ajar in the storm. Out into the blinding rain, the next unearthly flash and barrage from above, ear-splitting. The waves were enormous, great, towering, white-crested monsters tearing into the cove and splintering into foaming fragments on the rocks.

He saw her, her white nightdress visible against the black intensity of the towering waves. She was walking out, the object held out in front of her like an offering to the raging sea which swirled towards her. In a moment she was down in the current, the under-tow dragging her from him. He ran shouting into the waves, soaked by the rain and sea, towards her rolling form. But with him too were two figures in oilskins wearing sou'westers in the teeming water. Two fishermen had seen her and ran along the beach at an angle to his own progress. One, getting his large arms round her first brought her to the surface, her face white in the crack of the lightning flash but strangely serene, unaware, her eyes closed, the object she clutched unbroken, held to her chest by a tight grip.

*

The next day dawned white and misty. The storm had blown away eastwards, but the good weather had been broken.

The local GP had been excellent. She lay still, her breathing shallow, but she was safe. In the comfort of the bed her corn-coloured hair lay out on the pillow around her – she was dry again and warm. She would sleep safely for most of the day with the sedative he had given her. James sat on the bedside. All the others had gone. He eyed the ship in its bottle which lay in his hands. A harmless-looking thing. He turned it over, scrutinising the name on the stern, so intricately, lovingly painted. Such very fine workmanship. He saw that name ... *The Naiad*, the name she had repeated over and over before she finally lost consciousness.

He made his decision. He descended the stairs. The hotelier's wife was willing to stay with her. He took the parcel with him.

The morning was fruitless. His enquiries of a one handed antique dealer drew a blank. No one knew of him.

By lunchtime he was leg-weary with tramping the narrow alleyways – but no shop was to be found. It was as if he had never existed, but he certainly had. James knew that.

He had lunch on a tray in their room, but Sarah hadn't moved and the hotelier's wife said she would stay the afternoon, which was very good of her.

He went to the harbour record office and there it was. With no difficulty he had found it, *The Naiad*: 'Sloop of war laid down in 1776, built with speed for the war, manned locally and sent out in bad weather, lost with the whole crew, at the harbour's mouth, in the raging surf'.

Bare facts, but enough. The local parish records would have more. Armed with the other name he could trace it exactly.

His search took him through several people to a square white house in its own grounds at the back of the town. The door was opened by one of those splendid ladies who wear tweeds and brogues all year round and have their glasses on a cord around their neck.

'Mrs Cadwallada?'

'Indeed I am, and you must be Dr Strathearn. How do you do!' A very firm handshake.

'The vicar told me to expect you. So terribly sorry to hear about your wife's accident. I trust she is resting well?'

'Yes, thank you.'

He was shown into the drawing room. She sat opposite him, the inevitable black Scottie dog nosing his hand. His eyes lighted upon the documents Mrs Cadwallada had already looked out.

'It's a fascinating study. The WI have done an awful lot of work on the archives over this last year, and, you see, it all has its uses!' She smiled at him, and he warmed to her.

'Now.' She placed her glasses on her nose, lifting her chin to gaze at the open parish record books for the appropriate year.

'I've looked out the records of the loss of *The Naiad*. Poor young men – so many of them lost in sight of their sweethearts too – awful thing the sea.'

He didn't feel he could comment.

'Now you wanted Robert Shalacoe, didn't you?' She ran her finger down the lists.

'Yes, he's here all right. Robert Shalacoe, aged nineteen, he was a lieutenant.' James could have kissed her, but thought better of it.

'All the bodies that were found were brought up to the churchyard but some of them weren't found apparently.'

She looked up at him with her piercing intelligent eyes.

'Ah yes, there's more here … Now, I knew the name rang a bell. We did this section in the spring, and I remember then thinking what a gruesome little story it was.'

James's heart began to beat faster.

'Robert Shalacoe was one of the last to be seen alive. He was hanging in the rigging for some hours. His hand had been caught in the shrouds, but eventually the waves pulled him loose. His hand came off at the forearm – the only part of his body they recovered from the wreckage was that one hand. It was still tied to a spar when the pieces were washed ashore. Now I've got something else here somewhere … where is it?' She rustled through some papers on a small side table, extracting a sheet of neat handwriting.

'You see – it all comes in useful. He had a sweetheart, a Sarah Pendrith, who watched it all happen from the cove.'

She stopped.

'Are you all right, Dr Strathearn?'

'No, I mean, yes, perfectly, do carry on. It's just that that was my wife's name before we were married.'

'How very singular.' Mrs Cadwallada put a finger to her mouth and gazed at him through her spectacles.

'Yes, well.' She scanned the page.

'There was some argument between the vicar at the time and Miss Pendrith about what should happen to the hand. He wanted it buried with the other remains of course, but she said she wanted it. What a strange sad story, don't you think?'

He nodded. It was a sad little tale. 'There is a note about the argument and some letters. If you'd like to look at them? She writes that all she has of her loved one is a lock of his long golden hair. It is all too sad, don't you think? Even so many years later.' For a moment she looked quite moved by it.

'They were engaged to be married apparently.' She returned

to herself and scanned the pages for some moments.

'There's no record of what happened eventually. The grave of all those recovered is in the churchyard. I'll take you there later, if you'd like. I've got to take Ferdinand for his walk. Would you care for tea?'

The combination of trauma, detective work and gruesome history was enough, without polite tea added, so James declined but showed Mrs Cadwallada the model of *The Naiad*.

It was obvious that it belonged to the local museum and he promised that, with his wife's permission, he would donate it. He passed over his reasons, but said he thought that they would not want to take it home with them.

He made his way back to the hotel via the churchyard. Mrs Cadwallada had told him where to find the grave and he found it without much difficulty. It was well worn by two hundred years of salt wind, but he could make out the names under an inscribed heading.

The mortal remains of those
gallant men of this shore who
gave their all for God for King
and for Country

But there was no inscription for Robert Shalacoe.

Perhaps a hand wasn't worth mentioning as 'mortal remains' but he thought it ought to have been if that was all that had been recovered.

James felt satisfied with his day. He was tired, mentally and physically, but he felt satisfied that he'd laid the ghost – or whatever it was, some strange genetic strain, some lost race memory, he didn't know how to describe it – but with his wife safe and the mystery at least most part solved they simply wouldn't come to this place again. It would make a fascinating story for his friends, even a bit of psychical research. But he wouldn't tell Sarah, not yet anyway.

One thing he knew, the ship in its bottle would go to the local museum where it belonged, and where it could evoke no such uncanny reactions in the present day lives of real people.

He was able to be with Sarah when she awoke, and although dozy she could take some nourishment and receive visitors, the two local fishermen and the local doctor.

By 10.30 she was again ready to rest and James was certainly only too eager for bed – purely to sleep.

They didn't talk much of the night before. Sarah could remember almost nothing and he passed it off as an over-excited brain – too many major events too quickly, and so on.

He went to bed content, the ship in its bottle safely wrapped up in its parcel on his side of the bed. Sarah hadn't even asked after it.

*

It was in the depths of the night that he was brought to consciousness. He knew something was wrong. Before even he had opened his eyes. The sounds of the storm and the cries of distress entered his dreams and the sight of white foaming water against a blackened sky.

He was awake to see the ship heeling over, the sea monstrous, surging forward, its sails flapping and billowing the ship crashed against the ragged vicious rocks. And superimposed, as if a mystic figure of some great sea goddess, Sarah stood above the chaos, hovering in the sky, her hands cupping the very storm, her eyes pale and unseeing illuminated by the tragedy before her, the ship and its men fighting for survival.

He couldn't focus his eyes, whether he was seeing something far off or near to, whether she was so incredibly malevolent in the sky or close to him.

The cries of distress were in the air all around and the sounds of the thunder groaning and the sea seething brought him upright and alert. But they were all there, distance and perspective all wrong. She held the scene in her hands as it heaved and crashed with myriad sounds of horror.

She was moving, moving away from him. He could now see clear the windows and the door. She was holding the ship in its bottle, carrying it out of the room, going again to the shore.

He bounded from the bed, catching her by the shoulder with a jerk. She awoke, the bottle falling from her hand to smash on the floor. Hundreds of pieces of glass and intricate crafts-manship splintered on the floor. She collapsed backwards onto the bed.

The sounds had all gone. In an instant the room had returned to normal, perspective, light and shade, solid normality.

James gingerly crossed the floor and turned the light on. Sarah groaned and sat up rubbing her eyes as if just awoken by the sudden flood of electric light.

The bottle was smashed beyond repair, the model broken into pieces. James knelt down to examine it. He picked over the pieces as Sarah leant over the edge of the bed to examine what he was doing.

The realisation dawned on him as he sorted through the wreckage, even with the amount of skill it had taken to con-struct, to whittle and refine the thing from which it had been constructed and even with his limited knowledge of anatomy, it was obvious what he was examining. Once out of its bottle and in pieces the fine details were revealed as bones and sinews, small, intricate bones – and the sinews of ... what? The sails of parchment flesh, the rigging fine locks of golden hair; they were the remains he had sought, the missing hand, fashioned thus by a young woman in her grief – it was all that she had of her sweetheart.

After a night without sleep James and Sarah were out at dawn onto the headland above the cove where they gave back the thing that had been parted for so long. How he would explain it to the museum and Mrs Cadwallada he wasn't sure, but he knew that this was really where it belonged.

They watched the place where it hit the sea for some moments in silence. Sarah looked at him.

'Did you try to find the old man who gave it to us?'

James smiled.

'Yes, but I don't think we ever will. You know that name over the door – I bet it was Robert Shalacoe. We've done him a favour, and he's done us one.'

'What's that?'

'I think he's convinced me to go into general practice.'

Bobby Shafto's gone to sea,
Silver buckles on his knee;
He'll come back and marry me,
Bonny Bobby Shafto!

VII

The Call of the Piper

Tom, he was a Piper's Son ...

Long before the new Faith was brought to the north, in the nightime of the year, that magical hinge of time, between the waning and the waxing of the light, a wandering minstrel would come uninvited and unheralded out of the blustery blackness and into the smoke-filled halls of the petty kings, and there he would play his pipes and lead them in the dance a'wassailing. He asked no payment for his story and stayed but little time, but he led them dancing with his sound and soon would go his way ...

Thus Henry had first heard of the Magic Piper and his fabulous pipes when he was very young, living in the north country. The other pieces of the story he picked up as he grew older when he visited, in holidays, from school. The old women would speak of it sometimes over their work in the kitchen. The beauty of the pipes and the promise extracted from the kings, to keep the memory of the pipes through the years, to guard them when he was gone ... How the Piper was paid by the best these poor folk could offer; not to him was tribute given, but to the pipes themselves, how they were decorated and carved and gilded and made gleaming, the only payment he would accept, at the hands of the craftsman for the kings. And as they became more beautiful the pipes would sound the more magical; how they healed and cured and were the font of bliss for those who heard them. The lame danced, the deaf were able to hear – but only for the space when the piper was among them. And when at last the Piper passed from mortal sight they put him to rest on a sacred hill, and protected

him with charms and spells and kept faith – into the years that
followed – forever.

Henry grew up, his parents died and he moved away from his
home in the far north, eventually arriving at the music college in
London, where he explored many musical forms from distant
lands and from ancient times. Sometimes amongst all these
things he would be reminded, notions of the power of music in
healing brought it back to his mind, and the ancient instruments
found illustrated in yellowing texts or carved in church decorations. But not only in serious pursuits, it would surface in his
mind at strange times, as when wassailing around the London
pubs, the drunken merriment striking some distant memory.

But it wasn't until a Christmas holiday in the north that he
again felt the real power of the tales. He had gone to stay with a
friend he had made, Malcolm.

They were out walking on the hills. It was a frosty pale
morning with the watery yellow sun only a little above the south
eastern horizon. They were walking along the Edge, a shoulder
of the high land overlooking a deep valley, the valley lost in
mist; and suddenly, there it was, the earthwork, an ancient
burial chamber a hump of earth cold and frost-covered against
the rolling mist. The gnarled trees on the summit, thrusting up
from the whitened ground like clenched fists angrily threatening
the pale empty sky.

'What an astonishing place.'

'Isn't it? I thought you'd like it. It's your scene more than
mine really. I come up here in the summer.' Malcolm smiled.
'Seeking what you'd call inspiration – don't often get much
though.'

Malcolm was too off-hand about it. Henry felt a little disconcerted, as he often did when their conversation turned to more
spiritual things. Malcolm seemed never to notice the Presence in
quite the same way as Henry. Henry frowned. He did like the
place and because of that somehow felt Malcolm's prosaic
speech somehow obtrusive, like swearing in church.

They crunched nearer across the stiff frosted ground. A silence
clung to it, speech was inappropriate.

'What's it called?' Henry's voice was hushed. They stood at its foot, looking up into the ring of ancient trees, almost as if they dared not enter.

'It's called Piper's Stump.'

Malcolm too had become quieter, more reverent for the ancient solitude of the place.

The mist moved wisping about the branches of the trees, obscuring their tops and making them look the more like fists. It was terribly cold.

'Has it a history?'

It was a stupid question. But Malcolm understood his meaning.

'It's supposed to be the burial place of some pre-Christian minstrel or something.' He had thrown off his reverent quietness, and moved, suddenly, climbing the side as if he were walking in some trimmed tame London common. Henry nearly cried out, 'Don't', but he couldn't think why.

'Maybe that's why it gives me inspiration. The vibes coming up through the ground.' He aped a mock ghostly voice and waved his gloved hands about.

'Don't do that.'

His friend stopped.

'Whyever not?'

'I don't know …' Henry looked up at him. He couldn't explain why – he just didn't think it appropriate.

'Just don't.'

Malcolm shrugged and moved away across the brow of the mound.

It was then that he thought he heard it, the screeching of a pipe, far distant, and unlike anything he had heard before, a haunting, strangely empty sound, trembling on the every edge of his hearing.

But Malcolm came crashing back across the frozen tussocks and the sound was gone.

Henry almost asked him if he'd heard anything, but decided not to. It wasn't something to share.

*

Henry found himself thinking of that sound, trying to recreate it in his mind, to re-hear it throughout the rest of the day and into the evening by the crackling drawing room fire. It was almost a yearning he had, yet it had been so fleeting, and was probably no more than the mournful wind in the branches. But the yearning remained.

Later, in his bedroom, he stood at the window for a long time. this wing of the house faced the hills. The Edge marched away westward. His eyes strained against the darkness, his mind far off from the room, among the cold brittle trunks of the ancient circle of oaks. He unlatched the window. It was a stupid thing to do – and he stood, his dressing gown wrapped around him, the wind whipping in, cold and biting. But his ears stretching their senses to their limits, searching, searching ... but nothing, no sound, but the screech of a far-off owl and the bark of a fox in the snow.

He got into bed and it was warm and comforting. The wind began to blow harder, in gusts around the ancient old house, rattling the window. He felt that he couldn't have locked it properly as it rattled and rattled, but by then he was too far in sleep and drifted away, as the other sound came whistling in through the cracks, plaintive and echoing, from far away and long ago.

The next morning he awoke amazingly bright. He felt unusually happy confident – and his senses seemed somehow enhanced. The harsh northern weather obviously agreed with him. He was early to breakfast.

'I took Henry to Piper's Stump yesterday.' Malcolm was conversational at breakfast. His mother looked up.

'Really, dear? Did you like it, Henry?'

'Yes, Lady Celia – it has a very particular quality ...' He sought for an adequate description.

'It's so lovely up there.'

His hostess smiled, and buttered her toast.

'Yes. I believe that particular piece of land is the most ancient in the family possession. We've held land here for centuries of course, but that stretch of the Edge ... I don't even know if there are any records. It's been ours for ever.' She continued spreading butter on her toast, nonchalant, unpretentious in the pretensions of high aristocracy.

Malcolm chipped in.

'Of course the family's been here for ever as well.' He looked around for some more coffee.

'*Burke's Peerage* has us as kings of these parts before the wretched Saxons came. Mind you, *Burke's Peerage* has Henry's family descended from Boadicea, so you can see it's pretty unreliable!'

Henry ignored Malcolm's flippancy. He had wanted to ask the question before, but it had seemed somehow unworthy. The morning seemed more suited to the prosaic.

'Has it ever been explored – you know – excavated?'

Malcolm's eyes widened in mock horror.

'My dear, you don't ask that question here. Whatever next! Mother, who invited this young man?'

His mother looked up from the other end of the table.

'Don't be tiresome, Malcolm.' And to Henry, 'Is he like this at college?'

Henry was a trifle embarrassed. He looked at his friend's grin.

'Only some of the time, Lady Celia.'

'Well, thank heavens we don't have to put up with it here.' She reached for another slice of toast.

'What he is referring to is an old family traditon that Piper's Stump should never be disturbed. It never has been excavated, and presumably never will, as long as the family hold the land.'

Malcolm leaned over squinting at him.

'A regular little feudal regime, arcn't we?'

His mother ignored him.

'The reason for the ban is known only to the head of the family – and the heir when he reaches maturity.'

'Do you realise, Mother, that I ought to know now. Maturity is eighteen nowadays but I suppose one can't expect this family to move with the times.'

'That, Malcolm, is the age the government has deemed to give you the vote. It certainly isn't maturity in your case, but there again I can't imagine twenty-one will be for you either.'

Malcolm winced theatrically.

'My mother's very sharp this morning, Henry. Do forgive us.'

'Malcolm ...' His mother's tone was severe. Malcolm subsided.

'Well, my birthday's only ten months away – so I'll know then, won't I? And as I'm the only offspring you've got it will be my responsibility to look after it.'

Malcolm's father had married in old age, as Henry knew. He realised now how much this kind of lineage must mean to him. He certainly wasn't a family man, spending most of his time in solitude in another part of the house, but obviously it was necessary for the family to beget a son to be heir ... Henry found these old families extraordinary.

He wondered how running a country estate would fit in with being a professional musician, but Malcolm would probably let the agent do all that side of things, very much as must happen in his father's case.

The rest of the holiday went well. The house at Christmas filled with visitors and laughter. Lord Glendower deigned to come down from his private apartments for a time. Getting elderly, Henry thought, and he wondered again about his light-hearted friend inheriting all this weight of tradition and responsibility.

He went again to the mound, set lonely and desolate as it had always been. He dared to step foot upon the hallowed ground and stood on the brow among the trees, but although he waited there, alone, no music came haunting him. And he wondered if it had all been fancied, his childhood tales coming back to him. He knew then where he had heard of the Piper, laid to rest in an earthen mound. And he started back to the party and the laughter down at the house, trudging away from the tree-encircled stump. The wind rose suddenly, through the trees on the Edge, desolate and alone – and he felt he heard ... he turned to gaze again ... he felt he heard for an instant the echo of a sound, the jingling prancing through the trees, the procession that followed the illusive strain of the pipe ... But there was nothing, only the moaning of the cold wind and the banking dark clouds to the west.

*

The year passed by. Henry and Malcolm saw as much of each other as their work permitted, but Henry didn't again visit the Glendowers at home.

Finals came and went. For all his flippancy Malcolm did passably well. Henry, with hard work rather than inspiration, gained merits. And then the hunt for employment. Henry had hoped for an orchestra but settled a while for peripatetic teaching. Malcolm went abroad, 'the latter day grand tour' he called it, and sent postcards to his friend that collected around the mirror in his suburban bedsitting room and cheered the rather dismal Advent term. Henry sent a birthday card in November.

The invitation arrived in early December, just as Henry had begun to wonder what to do for his Christmas holiday. Malcolm was to be in London on his way north, so they could have supper together and plan Christmas. 'If you can bear to drag yourself away at Christmas that is ...'

He was delighted by the prospect, and entered the rather plush hotel in high spirits. His friend was there, incongruously tanned in a December London, glowing with his old brightness, his teeth white against his bronzed face.

'Ho, shadow of my youth, why lookest thou so pale and woebegone?'

'I've been working for my living – that's what – to the most unresponsive load of ruffians you can imagine!'

They shook hands, genuinely pleased to see one another, and Malcolm led the way into the feast.

The conversation eventually turned to the ensuing holiday and it was settled that they would go up together. But there was much more to be asked. Malcolm's twenty-first birthday had come and gone; he would have had his interview with his father – the heir would know. Henry ventured the question. It wasn't until he came to ask it that he realised quite how much it meant to him, how much he had thought about the asking, and how much he dreaded the aristocratic reproof that would bar him access to the mystery.

But there was no reproof. Malcolm's eyes twinkled mischievously and he toyed with the coffee spoon.

'Do you realise that if I tell you you're the first "not of the blood" to know. It's a sacred trust, you know!'

The edges of his mouth twitched into a smile and he moved forward conspiratorially.

'It's an awful lot of old eyewash.'

'Oh, Malcolm!'

He tried to sound the reprimand, but he didn't feel it. He was going to be told – he knew it. Malcolm was going to share the secret.

'Well … it's not really very interesting anyway. My father made a big fuss about it of course but you can never take anything he says seriously; he doesn't believe any of it himself.'

Henry was impatient. For some reason he desperately wanted to know. It had been something in the music he had heard that haunted him, something of the place had stayed with him. He knew that Malcolm didn't feel these things but it was a yearning he himself felt strongly, quite unlike anything he had known before.

Malcolm called for more coffee. Henry didn't know whether he was playing with him, sensing his desire to know and toying with him. It would be like Malcolm. He didn't take anything seriously, especially things sacred. It had always been like that at college, his aristocratic scoffing at the spiritual. The thought crossed his mind, 'He's not worthy of the knowledge'. Henry was surprised at his own anger of thought. He was thinking about his closest friend – and yet he so wanted to know about something that friend owned – that the friend alone had a right to – and that he was going to share out of friendship. But the thought arose again, almost loud in his mind, 'He isn't worthy of the guardianship'; as if spoken to him by another voice.

Where he got the idea of guardianship from he could not imagine.

With some effort he ignored the thought. He put it out of his mind by conscious effort, like turning the page on an unwanted chapter of a diary.

The coffee came and was served, and the waiter padded away across the deep pile carpet.

'Apparently this has been handed down from father to son for generations. God knows when it started, but my father says it comes from a time when we were kings.' He shrugged his shoulders. 'Piper's Stump is the burial place of a wandering minstrel. He was supposed to be in league with the gods of sunrise and springtime or something, and when he died in the hall of this ancestor of mine they made a big thing of it and buried him with full regal honours in a special tomb – his pipes with him – which is the only bit that interested me of course. If they are there still they would be a fascinating find, a priceless piece. Anyway there's some nonsense about the Piper's resting place bringing honour and riches on the house as long as we are the guardians.'

The word struck Henry as odd; extraordinary that he should have used the same word to himself just before he was told.

'There's something about a curse as well. All good spooky movie stuff. If we allow the Piper to be disturbed the House will fall. I suppose it's the family rather than the house. I wouldn't mind the insurance if the house fell down. It's not the original anyway. I think the present hall is the only bit that's medieval with the minstrels' gallery – but the rest is a Victorian Gothic, so it's hardly likely to be involved in ye olde curse, is it?'

He smiled his smile, incorrigible in his scepticism.

'That's it really. Give or take a few dire warnings from the Pater, who can't possibly believe any of it any more than I do.'

Henry felt distinctly odd, as if he shouldn't know, as if it really were sacrilege – which was foolish of course. But somehow it was wrong for Malcolm to speak so lightly of it.

He felt he wanted to make him appreciate the heritage more somehow. If only he could get Malcolm to hear the strange empty music that he had heard – to wonder a little.

'I know something about this ...' He spoke not really meaning to.

'Do you? I thought it was all supposed to be secret – just shows, you can't trust anyone – not even in the best families.'

He smiled, and drank some more coffee.

'No, not your side of it. But I've heard about the Piper – I bet it's the same one. It was when I was small – you know I grew up in the north – well there was this story of the magical piper with the fabulous pipes which would charm people ...'

'Sounds like an early version of the Pied Piper of Hamelin.'

'Yes it does a bit. But the Piper wouldn't accept any money for his music so they gave gifts to the pipes – you know, sort of embellished them with jewels and gold and carving, that sort of thing.'

'What, like the Nordic harpists? That sort of game?'

'Yes, I suppose so. There would have been a link with the Norse culture then, so I expect that is what it was.'

Malcolm sat forward in his seat.

'What a find something like that would be. What a wheeze – can you imagine – if we dug it up?'

The two things happened at once. There was a sudden gust of cold air as if one of the waiters had opened a window. It ruffled the table cloth, upsetting Henry's coffee, but the other thing had more effect. Henry clutched at his ears trying to stop the sound, the screech that must have gone through everyone in the room. The searing pain of the high pitched notes which seemed to tear at his eardrums making his mind reel. His eyes screwed tight – closed – he shook his head to rid himself of the sound and then it was gone. Through the tears in his eyes he saw the astonished face of Malcolm opposite, apparently unaffected by the terrible sound, and then, as he regained equilibrium – the faces of others in the room turned towards him, their conversations interrupted. And the head waiter quietly padding across the carpet ...

'Is anything wrong sir? Can I get you anything? Do you require assistance?'

*

It was a foolish, stupid enterprise. Henry could see Malcolm's back in the torchlight of the tunnel, the scraping of the spade against the soil. It was madness even from a physical point of view – digging so deep into virgin earth; but Malcolm had been proved right. The stout intertwined roots of the oaks above had kept the tunnel from caving in.

But the other consequences ... Henry didn't dare think. It was so stupid of him to let Malcolm persuade him, everything against any judgement he would make. The wind howled cold outside the tunnel entrance, the night was dark; Henry knew that this was the only time they could work undetected. He cursed his involvement, and the silver-tongued entreaties of his friend.

The noise of the spade suddenly sounded different; it had hit wood. 'We've got to the wall.' The thud of the metal against old rotten wood.

'It should be comparatively easy to get through now.'

The thud again, as the sharp metal sank deep, the grinding splintering as he pulled it loose again.

He had pleaded with him not to go ahead – but it had been useless. His mind had been set upon it – and he was a guest in the house, and Henry valued his friendship.

There was a grinding splintering as the rotten old wood came to pieces.

'Hold the torch up – I can't see a thing.'

He held the torch up. The beam cut through the hole, into the darkness. They gasped, recoiling back – for there – staring at them – was a face.

The torch being dropped, they rummaged frantically, shaking, shaken, seeking the lost light. Malcolm had it again, the beam cutting through the hole into the blackness beyond. But it wasn't a face of course, and it hadn't been propped up. It had been a trick of the moment somehow. They had expected bones of course; it had been the shock of seeing a whole body. How they had imagined it to be sitting up, just inside, beyond the wall – they couldn't tell – it was as if it had been waiting for them. It was of course lying down, as it should have been, feet towards them, its head on a pillow of stone. But it was incredibly well preserved. Even remnants of clothing still clung to the emaciated limbs, the great skull still bore the remnants of flesh, the eye cavities deep, but in their depths something shrivelled, the remains of eyes Henry assumed.

They clambered through the hole, still shaken; fear and anticipation mixed, for there, by its side, shining in the light of the torch, lay the musical instrument – so delicately carved, so exquisite in its fine gold-work and dark gleaming gems. It was like an etched instrument seen in Chaucerian woodcuts, but incalculably older – a remnant from a forgotten age, an actual instrument of the Dark Ages, untouched for nearly one and a half millenia. And they were the first to see it, clutched as it was in the cobwebbed and sinewed hands of the long dead minstrel.

'Come away, Malcolm – leave it be. We've seen it – that's enough.'

'Don't talk wet.' He sounded angry in the dark – not himself, not the usual flippant voice of lightness, but something else, something had infected him in the dark place.

They stood a long time in the cramped little chamber – their only light falling on the priceless instrument, and the fingers that held it so tightly.

Henry moved suddenly, he snatched the torch from his friend and shone it further up the body, to the head. It had been a slight movement, a fraction of sound that had arrested his attention. It was the wreath of dried leaves, around the head; they had moved. The torchlight lit them. He was right – there had been an almost undetectable change, one or two of the dried leaves had moved, stirred slightly, looking perhaps a little more like living ivy.

'The wreath – it's moving.'

'Nonsense. It's probably the air getting to it – the leaves are crumbling away.'

But, as they looked, it didn't appear like that. Rather, the fragile skeleton seemed to be opening again, filling out; almost as if a kind of life was beginning to return to it.

Henry stared at it in the white torchlight. The head too seemed slightly different, the dried tissue of flesh and sinew slightly less brittle – very slightly, so very slightly more like white, living skin, clinging, like lichen, to the lifeless bone of the long dead skull.

'I'm going, you can stay if you like but I'm going ... we shouldn't have come. It's wrong. We must leave it here ... Malcolm.'

His friend turned sharply in the darkness, the torchlight shining up between them, casting shadows upward making his face so different.

'If you go now you can leave for good! It's my property and I'm having it. You're only a stranger – remember that – you don't belong. You're not of the blood!'

Henry staggered back in the dark. The vehemence unnerved him; already taut with fright and misgiving it was too much for him.

He muttered a few words of apology and clambered for the hole in the chamber wall. With elbows and knees he clawed his way forward, out from the chamber and along the tunnel.

The air was fresh and cold – the frosty stars lit the sky in a great arch of whiteness. He breathed in the normality of the night, and set off for the house. Not a backward glance, not a thought but to be away and safely.

*

It was a shock to stumble through the front door and find everyone still up, but of course it was not very late, and they were watching television or playing board games by the great log fire in the hall. He could hear someone playing the piano through the open doors that led to the drawing room. All the sights and sounds of a country house gathering at Christmas time, no discord, no sinister shadows, no fear ... irrational was the fear that clung to him, like the smell of that dark little chamber.

After taking his hat and coat off – and pulling himself free of his boots he stood by the hall fire warming himself.

'Oh, do you hear, we've got carol singers.'

A young woman was standing by one of the long windows that looked out onto the drive, and was peering out into the night. He could hear the singing from where he stood – but also the sound he had come to dread. They were no ordinary carol singers.

A cluster of people gathered by the windows staring out, and as they did the sound jingled nearer – the strange empty, plaintive singing with the Piper at its head.

Several of the men cupped their hands to the window, peering out, trying to glimpse the singers.

'That's not a carol,' one said.

'They're wassailers – can't you hear?'

Henry stood back from the others, but he could hear them coming, singing along the dark lanes of the night, jingling and prancing through the trees, the sound flowing out behind them, like their tattered raiment. Following, following the pipes that had played them down the years ...

'I can't see anything.'

'No, look, there they are ... coming down the drive.'

'I'll open the door – we'll be able to hear them better.'

Before he could stop them the great oak door was unlatched and blew back with such force it caught them all unawares. The great cold blast of icy wind howled through the house, upsetting wineglasses and board games. The log fires blazed up and spat, hissing like a basket of frightened cats.

And there, in the doorway, stood Malcolm, hollow-eyed and breathing heavily, a bundle held tight to his chest. He pushed through the clustered group.

The wind faded away and they scrambled to the door and looked out past Malcolm – into the empty dark night.

'Well, where are they?'

'That's strange. They were coming round the curve in the drive just now.'

'Did you see the wassailers, Malcolm?'

'What wassailers?'

Malcolm asked the question with his back to them, regaining

his breath after the long run to the house.

Henry could see his face, the look in his eyes, the clutched fingers holdings its bundle.

'They were there just now, must have been on your very heels.'

'There weren't any wassailers. There's no one out there – not a living soul.'

Henry put out his hand to touch his arm but Malcolm struck it off and glared at him. The look conveyed almost hatred. Malcolm walked away from him and trudged up the wide staircase.

The group by the door closed it again and drifted away, the others got back to their re-assembled board games or had their drinks cleared up and settled back into other armchairs again. But Henry sensed a difference. It had grown strangely cold in the house, something had changed.

And there was a change, if only incidental to the life of the house. The next few days saw Malcolm different, in his attitude to Henry at least, shunning him, ignoring him, talking past him in conversation. And something else too, he had become peculiarly jumpy. The slightest noise would have him up and looking about, asking others if they had heard it too. He always gravitated to the largest group, and quite obviously elbowed his way in, to be among the others.

On the second night there was a fearful storm that raged and buffeted against the house. Henry was kept awake well into that night, with the sounds of the tempest raging around him, and the small sounds – the crashes and bangs of slates coming off the roof, and chimney pots falling – almost as if the fingers of the storm were trying to gain access into the building. He fancied he heard the skirmishing, prancing through the night, the jingling of bells and the empty laughter of the dancers, but he couldn't be sure through the howling of the wind.

The park was desolate in the morning; great branches had been torn from the trees along the drive, the terrace scattered with broken debris from the roofs. By lunchtime the news reached them that two of the oaks of Piper's Stump had blown down and the stump itself partly demolished.

Lord Glendower was distraught and forbade any guests from visiting the Stump to see. He inspected it himself as the day worsened again and the freezing rains that followed the gales came sweeping in along the Edge. He personally supervised the repair work and the dismantling of the broken oaks. The men working on in the worsening conditions.

Henry wondered about the tunnel workings that had undermined their roots, and how they must have weakened the structure.

But the others in the party, unaware of his personal doubts, stood in groups in the gloom of the house and passed worried words about the wisdom of the old man to stay out so long in the bitter driving rain and icy wind. He refused all sustenance until well into the night – when the job was done – and he returned soaked and really frozen, his old hands cracked and bleeding where he had helped the workman, his lips blue with cold, working feebly, an anxiety in his eyes.

Malcolm was not to be seen for most of that day. His part of the house had suffered most from the previous night's gales, so much of the roof above his bedroom had been damaged that it let in water. He complained that the workmen were busy repairing Piper's Stump when the house itself was falling down, and he spent most of his time moving his belongings to another room.

The New Year's planned festivities were cut short, Lord Glendower had been too old and too frail to withstand the exertions, and was confined to his bed. The party lost its zest and began to break up the day after Boxing Day, some guests leaving early; others, who had planned to go soon anyway, making their farewells as briefly as possible. As the winds began to howl again and Lord Glendower's health began to deteriorate a rather sad procession of cars began leaving the house. The whole thing bore the impression of finality; so suddenly had the change taken place, and so dreary the circumstances, that everyone seemed to leave in depression.

Henry had looked for Malcolm to make his farewells, but

couldn't find him. It was as if his friend had cut him off without a second thought. It was on the assumption that Malcolm would recover from his black mood that Henry left the house – little realising that he would never see his friend again.

*

The first newspaper reports of the family were perhaps to be expected. A few weeks into January Henry read Lord Glendower's obituary. He had apparently lingered for some weeks, but the strain had been too much for him. Henry wrote to the new Lord Glendower but received no reply.

The next reports of the family were far more dramatic with pictures on the front paper of the tabloids, and headlines proclaiming the disaster.

Henry first saw the pictures on someone else's newspaper held up in front of him on a tube train. At first he only vaguely recognised it, so changed was the appearance. It was the shape of the chimneys that he remembered and drawing closer to examine the picture of the wreckage he marvelled that anything like it could happen. The masses of broken stone and debris, the gutted windows and shell-like walls – all that remained of Castle Glendower, the massive structure brought to rubble. And then as the person refolded his newspaper he made out the headline: 'Country House Catastrophe – priceless treasures lost – young peer feared dead.'

He hurried back to his lodging with two newspapers under his coat. He had managed to glean some information before the rain forced the newspapers away. The family had been away for the Memorial Service and the terrible storms had raged around the house all the while buffeting the old building.

He got to his lodgings to find his landlady's television on in the sitting room. She called him to come and see. She knew of his acquaintance with the 'young lord' as she called Malcolm. She was intent with the kind of fascination on disasters befalling the wealthy and titled can engender. Henry found her prattle excruciating and he wrung his hands. But the news studio description gave way to an interview with one of the servants against a background of the wreckage, police still combing the mountains of rubble.

Henry sat on the arm of a chair; he vaguely recognised the elderly servant.

'I was in my quarters in the east wing when I first heard it, the sounds of the wind in the chimneys had been like howling music all the day – like pipes being played it was – but by the evening the rain and gale was so much that I could hear the timbers in the roof of the great hall beginning to creak. I went into the hall to see what was going on and great cracks had begun to appear in the tie beams. The roof was of stone.' The old man turned to look over his shoulders at the wreckage.

'It must have been pressing down on the beams for nigh on six hundred years. Well, there was nothing I could do so I got the others down to the Lodge and stayed up at the house to watch. I telephoned the young Lord Glendower and he said he would motor over straightaway. The gale was rising – and about 11.30 young Lord Glendower arrived. He drove right up to the front door although I warned him not to. He went in. He seemed in a terrible hurry, he said he had to return something. It would be all right he said, if he returned something. He said there was something very particular he wanted to get out. He sent me to get the other man from the lodge to help get some of the furniture out. I got back to the house at 11.45. I heard one of the beams beginning to go. The whole roof from where I was standing seemed to lurch sideways – the weight of the stone was too much with the gale behind it – and it began to give in and pushed the whole front wall out, its whole length, out into the driveway, completely covering the car. It was a terrible sound. I'll always remember it, it was like the *Titanic* going down, a great moaning crash it was, and the noises afterwards, the breaking and the crashing of small things inside, the great staircase giving way like thunder and the wind blowing through the broken mullions and the chimneys, it sounded like laughter. I didn't see young Lord Glendower after that. But they haven't found his body yet, although they've searched the wreckage of the house, moving the great broken beams and tons of stone. But if he do be dead, last of the line like he was, the family has died out as well.'

Henry had such mixed feelings about it. He wasn't really sure he was truly sorry, it seemed that some kind of justice had been done in a strange way for the old Lord Glendower had been the last of the true guardians. Malcolm had never really shared in the knowledge of one that was 'of The blood.'

The news items about the disaster held attention for some days, but finally public interest waned. The body was not found but Malcolm was assumed dead on the evidence of the servant.

After a suitable interval the estate came onto the market. It was broken up. The rest of the house, deemed unsafe, was finally demolished and its stone used for other buildings.

Some few years later Henry's eye was caught by a paragraph in the paper. It read:

Ancient Burial Mound opened – Glendower mystery solved.

On the fifteenth of August, the local antiquarian society of Glendower Park opened up the ancient tumulus known as Piper's Stump. The remains of a late Bronze Age burial were found, along with numerous exciting artifacts of the period. The famed pipes of the fable were alas not found, presumably long since decayed. But found in the small burial chamber along with the original body was found a far more recent corpse. This had been formerly identified as the remains of the last Lord Glendower, who mysteriously disappeared the night of the tragic loss of the historic family home. The body of Lord Glendower who had been a musician held in his hands what appears to have been the remains of an ancient musical instrument but it was too rotted to be properly examined before decaying.

Tom, he was a piper's son,
He learned to play when he was young,
But all the tune that he could play
Was, 'Over the hills and far away'.
Over the hills and a great way off,
The wind will blow my top-knot off.

VIII

All Is Not As It Seems

Little Red Riding Hood

For anyone who had not before visited Woolminster I should perhaps give some description. It appears, and indeed generally is, a sleepy and peaceful little cathedral city; indeed its only claim to city status resides in its episcopal seat, for in population and business it is now but a small market town set at the bridging point on the River Rayne below the high Wroxetshire downs and above the estuary marshes. The downs and the outlet to the sea were its twin reasons for existence – the town growing up around the great abbey church that had been central to the wool trade for the area. For centuries the great sheep flocks from the high downs had been yearly driven along the drove roads that centre upon the abbey, filling the streets and market with noise and bustle and bringing wealth to the abbot and his people.

The wool trade, from whence its name is derived, endowed the town with much prestige in days gone by and many grew rich here. Even after the dissolution of the monasteries they remembered the root of their success and gave of their prosperity to the now cathedral church, adding grandeur and beauty to the building itself and its adjacent houses, and also the school that grew up under its shadow. It is indeed one of the oldest choir schools in England, and with the reduction of monastic use the school took over some of the most ancient parts of the close and cloister.

It was to the school that I came, weary and confused, like an ancient pilgrim seeking rest from the frantic world, a rather pathetic victim of a world too hard. My love of music drew me

139

and my real love of teaching if only I were allowed to teach and not be harassed by the demands of discipline. And, I must admit it, there was that other thing: the innocence and yes, the beauty of these choirboys I had sat and watched and listened to. Their ethereal singing, controlled and disciplined in that beautiful building, was like heaven itself. And there was also that kindness I knew would be waiting for me. My uncle, long resident in the close of Woolminster, precentor of the cathedral choir, Canon Cedric. He had said there was a position available for a choirman. One of the young choirmen had had an unfortunate accident and had to be replaced. By coincidence he too had taught classics, so I was aptly fitted for the post. My uncle knew of my nervous breakdown but yet he made it all possible. He even made light of it, saying that the school was privileged in having so talented an academic. But the brilliance, such as it had been at Cambridge, had all fallen to nothing in my experiences in the classroom. He knew that too but did not speak of it.

As I passed along the High Street with its jumble of buildings, medieval to Georgian, I felt that some great incubus had lifted from my shoulders. Surely here, surely here among the ancient and beautiful buildings, I would find the peace for which my soul craved. Even though some ill-conceived modern shop-fronts had elbowed their way in, even though the railway station was modern and horribly reminiscent of the concrete and glass I had left behind, I felt I was coming home. The market square with its rather grand Georgian woolmarket and rising above all, the great cathedral church with its tower standing solid against the autumn afternoon sky, a great statement of security. I passed through the close gate into Canon's Walk. Number 12 I was looking for, as I had as a child visiting here, the ancient houses with their mullioned windows and small neat gardens, up to the front door. He had been waiting, and the door was as soon knocked upon as opened and his large shape and open-handed welcome were mine.

'Crispen, my dear boy, come in, come in. I have the kettle on for some tea.' And he spoke to me of things seemingly so quiet and gentle. The forthcoming great centenary service. The Septuacentenary he called it, seven hundred years since the building of the Minster, and he enthused about how busy they had all been this year preparing for the great occasion. How delightful it all was to my ears, somehow so removed from tensions, so far from the hostility that had left its marks on me. The serene Woolminster celebrating seven hundred years of peace and spiritual calm in its own so gentle provincial way.

Looking back on it all now, it seems there was so much certainty in my arrival, so much of a future burying oneself in the past. It's extraordinary how few things really are as they outwardly appear.

But I do not tell the story – and I must write these things down.

All had gone quite well apart from the difficulty over my trunk which had apparently got mislaid in transit. Arriving as I had done during the October Exeat I had time to settle in and meet colleagues before term resumed. I had my predecessor's room in a very ancient part of the buildings, linking directly to the Song School where we would practise daily. My predecessor had left most of his things, which were to be collected by his family I was told. It is hardly usual for me to borrow other people's things, but I was worried by the non-arrival of my trunk. It distressed me that I would not be properly dressed for meeting new people, and on finding that my predecessor must have been about my size the temptation to wear his suit was too strong for me. I asked the Headmaster his advice and he said he was sure Jeremy (my predecessor's name) would have no need of them, so I wore his tweed suit.

It was then that the first curious thing happened.

I had put the jacket on before going out for the evening to be introduced to the Dean, and put my hands in the pockets, when a strange darkness fell upon me. All of a sudden all the old dreads assailed me – almost as if they rose around me like a surging tide. As quickly as it had come it went again, passing on, I felt, bound for some other place, and in its wake a faint noise. I had slumped in my desk chair but I heard the sound carried away in the wake of the darkness, a chanting which died in a whisper into the walls of my chamber.

I still had my hand in the jacket pocket and was shocked to realise I had slightly torn the pocket seam in my fall. I withdrew my hand to inspect the damage and found that my fingers had closed around a folded piece of paper. I put it on the desk without further thought for it. My concern was with the jacket. A few stitches would repair it which I would accomplish on my return from the Deanery. It was an unpardonable thing to do when borrowing something, especially when doing so without the owner's knowledge. The Dean had been pleasant, my uncle making the introductions. He, too, said they were pleased to receive such an eminent scholar into their midst, and was pleased I'd come in time to join the choir for the great Septuacentenary.

'A cathedral doesn't celebrate its 700th birthday every day you know,' he said, and added that he thought I looked well, and was gentle; obviously my uncle had spoken to him about my illness.

I didn't dare mention the sudden recurrence, but did mention the torn pocket and how I had borrowed the suit without the owner's permission. The Dean seemed concerned to make me feel at ease and expressed his certainty that Jeremy's family would not mind. He seemed about to say more, but my uncle interrupted in what I thought a rather ungracious fashion, saying how well he thought the suit fitted – and how they wouldn't need another cassock as I was Jeremy's size. I thought I noticed a particular glance pass between them, but couldn't understand why it should be. Later, on my way back to my rooms, I went over the conversation again. I often do, to think if I have said anything untoward, and it occurred to me as strange that the Dean should have spoken of Jeremy's family not being upset rather than Jeremy himself, but it was just a mode of speech, I told myself. It was then that I realised that no one had told me of what accident had befallen him, and indeed why he was not expected back at the school.

On returning to my rooms I sat at my desk to write my diary

and discovered there the slip of discoloured paper, parchment it looked. I unfolded it having quite forgotten whence it had come.

It was an inscription written in Latin, in a childish hand with notation like a medieval chant. I realised immediately that it was from Jeremy's pocket, but my enthusiasm for transcribing got the better of me and I absently translated the words:

Illi quem terret male sanae mentis imago
Nuntius haec refero Sideoni Ieremiae:
'Huc tandem venias, ex isto corpore surge,
'Te nostris comitem salientibus adde catervis,
'Quaeque latent penitus, sero reserata patebunt:
'Spiritus ipse reget: diseadat debile corpus.
'Hue fuge quem terret male sanae mentis imago!'

I sat over the transcription for some time. It made no sense at all. I shivered violently and decided that autumn evenings probably affected an old building more than a new one and I decided to write my diary in bed where I could have a hot water bottle. The translation lay on the desk.

To him whom the image of an insane mind terrifies,
As a messenger I bear these words – to Jeremy Sideons:
'May you come hither at last, rise up from that body,
Join in as a companion in our dancing bands,
And what lies deeply hidden, will at last be revealed:
The spirit itself shall rule: let the feeble body depart.
Come hither you whom the image of an insane mind terrifies!'

*

The two days left before the boys returned were spent in settling in. My trunk arrived and I was able to pack Jeremy's clothes away. The school porter came to collect them and I asked him to forward a letter to my predecessor. I had written admitting my fault with the newly stitched pocket and the inexplicable loss of that scrap of paper. I had looked everywhere for it. I imagined it was an exercise he had set one of the boys. The old porter mumbled something about not being able to get the letter to him where he was, but I pressed it upon him and he left mumbling something about him not worrying about stitched clothes now, but I had met the type of man before and knew their complaining ways.

I spent some of my time exploring the ancient school buildings which included some very fine medieval monastic architecture. As something of a student of architecture I took my sketch pad with me, just making occasional jottings of what caught my interest, so I could return later and make better drawings.

The Song School was a particularly extraordinary two storey octagonal room abutting my own quarters, indeed there was even a peep window from the back of what was now my wardrobe through which one could observe the Song School below. When in the Song School itself I tried to find the little opening, but couldn't see it. It was high up in the recesses behind some carvings which stood on a plinth around the room just under the roof. I don't expect I would have noticed them, were I not looking for that peep window, but once I had spied them my interests were aroused. They were obviously a sort of story, read from left to right with figures and animals.

I was making some sketches of what I could see of the carvings when my uncle found me.

'Crispin, dear boy, whatever are you doing here? I thought I had entirely lost you.' He stood at my elbow looking down at the sketches. I looked at him to see if he liked them but saw a frown hover on his brow. He looked up at the carving I was copying. He stood with his hands held behind his back rocking on his heels, a habit he had had for as long as I could remember. Yet his normal placidity appeared a little distracted. It worried me, I didn't want to do anything to displease him, but he appeared so.

'What are you doing that for?' The question was a little sharp having an edge to it, but before I could answer he had moderated his tone.

'I was wondering whether you'd care to come for supper, it being the evening of the boys' return. I'm sure I can provide something worthy of the occasion.'

He smiled at me, the frown lifting from his bushy eyebrows; atwitch again with gentle intent. It was so kind a thought I was indeed beginning to be anxious. His glowing fireplace and untidy old house were an ideal refuge.

'I just wanted to get this done – and then I'd love to come.' I didn't want to delay him. I tried to think of a distraction.

'What do you think of these carvings, Uncle?' The frown appeared again, but then a return to his normal self. He stuck out his lower lip, bending low over the sketches, and squinted at them. He turned his head this way and that and then cast an eye up at the carvings.

'I've never really studied them carefully.' He looked up – half apologetic, taking the drawings.

'To tell you the truth I'd never noticed them before, Crispin.'

He coughed and stopped. He suddenly grinned, giving his face a far younger aspect.

'But they're very good sketches.' He shuffled the papers.

'I suppose they're meant to represent shepherds and the flocks, are they?'

'Yes ... I should think so. Do you see, it's like a frieze? There's that figure who is obviously leading and he's not a shepherd. He looks to me like an abbot.'

My uncle gave me a quick sudden glance – which held in it more than I could read. He had been acting uncharacteristically since first realising what it was I was doing. But his only verbal comment was a slow 'Yes ...' and he turned on to the next.

'And that must be a monk, following. I wish I could get up nearer. The carving looks really quite intricate but one can't really tell from down here. Then there's a shepherd – and the sheep – oh and, do you see by the abbot's gown, just visible? It must be a sheep dog ... or something like one. I'd have to get a ladder to have a closer look.'

He actually gave a nervous start at the suggestion.

'Oh, I wouldn't bother to do that my boy. No, no, I would have thought these were quite good enough, you know. There are some far better carvings elsewhere in the cathedral.' He noticed my crestfallen and moderated look.

'Of course, if you really want to look at them, we must get Geoffrey Simmons to give you a hand. He's just retired from being head verger. You'll like Geoffrey – he'd be glad to help. There's nothing that Geoffrey doesn't know about the cathedral buildings. You mustn't go up a ladder here on your own. The floor is too slippery. You might fall and have a nasty accident.' He looked down at a spot on the floor beneath the carving.

'Well, I wonder if he'd be able to help with that then.' I pointed to what had been taxing my skills.

'It's rather dark in that corner, so one can't be quite sure what it is, but there's something else – following on. Do you see it?'

My uncle peered into the gloomy recess at the opposite end of the frieze, but shook his head.

'No, I can't make it out. Is it another sheepdog?'

'I don't think so.' I looked down from the carving to the few lines I had drawn on the sketch pad.

'No, it's too big – and, do you see? – it stands too high as if it's standing on two legs ... yet ...'

'Yet what?' My uncle's attention had obviously begun to wander towards his supper arrangements.

'And yet one of the only bits I can make out is a snout – with teeth – I suppose it could be a dog.'

*

As good as his word my uncle had invited his friend Geoffrey Simmons to supper with us.

He was a charming old man and talked much about the cathedral history. Once or twice I tried to ask about the carvings in the Song School but my uncle managed to interrupt again, as he had done at the Deanery two days before, I began to suspect his hearing was beginning to be affected by his age, not quite catching conversations.

But I was puzzled to overhear a small exchange between the

two when I was returning to the room from the lavatory; the verger's voice first:

'I think you should tell him about the carvings ... has he seen the inscription ...'

'It can't be of any account, Geoffrey. The Abbot's laid to rest, we both know it, it's all a coincidence.'

*

The boys had returned and I thrilled at the experience of singing with them. They seemed such gentle creatures, truly courteous and so dedicated to their music; serious-minded they would wait and watch the choir-master at rehearsals with those wide intent blue eyes. I was astonished how beautiful they were, but I had to be wary, I knew my own weakness for them. They made such a spectacle filing out across the close with their red habits on. On colder evenings they would put the hoods up and look like a file of red-gowned monks wending their way to prayers.

They simply weren't like other boys I had met – and teaching them was a delight. They were particularly enthusiastic about Medieval Church Latin and would tax my knowledge and sent me scurrying to check things they seemed to know instinctively.

I had been told to be wary of the first few days.

'They are summing you up,' other members of staff told me and intimated that they could be little demons.

But I could not fail to be open and share my thoughts and feelings with them. They would flock around me, uniformly beautiful with their blond hair and blue eyes. I could not imagine a more beautiful choir in all of England, and they seemed so intent to make friends and to please me. I suppose they recognised my affection for them and responded.

My uncle laughed when I told him at tea in Geoffrey's house one day. He said that he had heard I had worked a miracle, apparently they had been awful to my predecessor, quite the epitome of horrid schoolboys.

I warmed at this information. One is always pleased to hear one is thought of more highly than a predecessor, and I had suffered much recently of the opposite.

So my affection for them grew.

My uncle said that others too had noticed how changed they were since my arrival. It was the talk of the Close apparently, how angelic they had become.

Only Geoffrey, the elderly verger, seemed unhappy about the liaison. His expression was dark as I spoke of these things – and I saw him cast a warning glance at my uncle, but my uncle, on the contrary, revelled in his amusement at what he described as 'Crispin's Miracle.'

It did not make me dislike Geoffrey Simmons, but I was concerned lest he doubt my good intentions with the boys. I strove to point out that my interest was entirely innocent.

It was a week or so later that I first heard the chanting late at night.

At first, for a night or two, it came and went, as if in a dream, and that is what I thought it was. But the specific sound and form of words did ring a bell in my memory that I couldn't quite place …

On the third night I was actually awakened by the sound. The steady rising and falling of an ancient chant. I could hear it muffled. I got up in the dark, trying to trace the sound, and found myself beside the door into my wardrobe. I opened the door carefully and realised immediately why the sound came to my room. It was in the Song School. I looked at my wrist watch, the luminous dial told the hour at ten past one.

I pushed into the little space and looked through the peep-window. It was a strange sight indeed. In candlelight the boys of the choir were assembled around a circular pattern drawn on the floor. They stood with their red gown hoods up, and each held a candle. They stood in a circle in the circumference of the pattern – and chanted. I tried to catch the words. It was obviously a form of Latin. I couldn't make it out. But I recognised where I'd heard it before. It was in my room when I had just arrived. I began to tremble, the dark, being aroused late at night, the curious behaviour; I found it all so unnerving. They stood still as I watched, but there was a movement, a small movement, on the shiny marbled floor. Something moved over the surface, something small that slid across the tiles. It glittered in the candlelight, as it moved from one figure to another. They sang. It was something made of silver. With a surge of mounting anxiety I recognised what moved – moved of its own volition, across the chalked circle. It was an upturned silver chalice.

The tide must have encompassed me, as I awoke in the entrance to the wardrobe, the clothes fallen about me, a clutter of hangers and jackets. It was still dark. I looked at my watch. The luminous hands pointed to the time. 12.55 – nearly one o'clock. I struggled up and looked out through the peep-window. The Song School was dark and silent.

*

'What a very singular story, my boy.' My uncle smiled and offered me another cup of tea.

'Don't you think so, Geoffrey?' The old verger didn't smile. He wore the same dark expression I had seen before. He picked up a sandwich and gazed at it – unseeing.

'I've heard more peculiar stories, Canon.'

It wasn't what he said, it was the way that he said it that seemed to affect my uncle. He looked up at the verger his smile gone.

The old verger looked at me and said, almost as if to continue the conversation with my uncle.

'The date of the Song School you wanted, Mr Crispin, was fourteenth century. It was one of the first of the monastic buildings, and was built as a wool assize under the first abbot ...' He looked across at my uncle who seemed strangely affected by the words. He stared and shook his head.

'Boys will be boys, Crispin ... initiation rites – they've always been part of boarding school life. I told you they could be naughty ... even if it was real ... even if it wasn't – your imagination, which is I know what you half suspect.' It was only a glancing reference to my illness, but it found its mark. I was wounded that he should mention it. It was so unlike him even to intimate. But he looked unusually flustered and seemed almost to use it as ammunition to shoot down my questioning.

'And even if it were some kind of naughtiness ... I'm sure there is no evil in them.'

And then to his old friend.

'Geoffrey – I'm sure there's no evil. They may be mischievous but not evil ... it can't be ... not again ...' He trailed off, uncertain, shaking his head. But I felt then that I shouldn't talk to him about it, even though it made me feel wretched and isolated. My fears began to stir again. I couldn't speak to the boys either. I valued their friendship. They would think I had been spying on them if I told them what I'd seen ... and it wasn't true.

The cathedral bell began to ring.

'Ah, evensong.' My uncle looked up at the clock on the mantelpiece.

'Quarter to five, time to get going.' He stood up and clapped his hands together.

'Doesn't your arm itch to be pulling the bell rope at this time each day, Geoffrey, as it has done all these years?'

It was, even to me, an unconvincing performance – a pathetic cover for unspoken worries, or perhaps they were fears.

Evensong over, the boys filed out of the choir stalls and headed off in their neat columns of red towards the school buildings. They weren't supposed to acknowledge anyone as they passed, but several smiled at me, showing their white healthy teeth. And then there was Rupert, the head chorister, with his blond hair swept back and his perfect complexion. He smiled unashamed at his pleasure in seeing me and my heart warmed. I smiled back, but then looked down – embarrassed at the openness.

Geoffrey Simmons came up to me where I stood watching them. I greeted him.

'They're like Little Red Riding Hoods, don't you think, dressed up like that?' I didn't refer to the teatime conversation

– it was too embarrassing. He looked after them.

'Very likely, sir,' he said and then, with a touch of urgency in his voice: 'They'll be at supper in five minutes, Mr Crispin. Do you want to go and look at that there carving you were on about? There's something I want to show you.'

I couldn't quite see what the boys being out of the way had to do with it, but I readily agreed. It had been Mr Simmons who had taken me seriously earlier in the afternoon. He led the way quickly yet, it occurred to me, somehow surreptitiously. He looked from right to left to check that we were not observed before opening the creaking door to the Song School. He was well prepared; he already had a ladder lying outside the room, which we manoeuvred in with some difficulty and turned around to lean it up against the appropriate wall.

I realised I hadn't got my original drawings and said I would only be a few moments. I was encouraged by his interest, and was very quick – although my rooms abutted the Song School on the second storey it was quite a way around to get to them, along a stone vaulted corridor and up a spiral staircase and back again along a winding passageway.

When I was in my room I thought I heard a muffled cry, a few words, something like 'be careful there, boy' and then a note of fear, 'No, boy – don't do it!' I couldn't detect from where it had come, perhaps outside on the field.

I must have been five minutes, no more, but when I returned there was something of a commotion. The school porter rushed past me and a gaggle of boys pushed each other at the entrance to the Song School. The Headmaster was there looking red-faced and worried.

'Oh, Crispin, Mr Simmons has had an accident. He was up a ladder in here for some reason and the ladder must have slipped. It's an awful occurrence.' And over his shoulder to another master who was clearing the gawping boys from the door, 'Exactly what happened to young Jeremy – it really is quite a dreadful coincidence.'

I pushed through, my mind in a whirl, uncertain what I would find.

Geoffrey Simmons' prone twisted body lay on the polished floor, the ladder lying some way off. He had a deep cut on his forehead which oozed thick blood. He looked death pale ... but I could see no other injury.

Matron came bustling through the throng as two masters called the boys away and got them into some kind of order. I looked up as she came through the crowd, and noticed how all the boys at the front of the throng were members of the choir, unlike the others who pushed and gawped they were standing placid, their faces emotionless – like masks – their blue eyes large, intent.

Geoffrey Simmons moaned. The Matron knelt by him, feeling his pulse.

'Thank God,' she whispered.

'At least he's alive.' She looked up at me. 'Not like the other one.'

The choirboys turned abruptly on their heels – almost like a regimented movement, and filed away, under the direction of the masters, unspeaking. I was left with an impression of that emotionless blue-eyed stare, and the Matron's words, but I was called out of my reverie – a stretcher had been brought. He was to be taken away, an ambulance had been called, he would be taken to the Cottage Hospital.

*

I couldn't get that strange stare out of my mind, but when I encountered the boys at the special choir rehearsals for the forthcoming great service they were their normal, smiling, beautiful selves ... I saw an increasing amount of them as the great service drew nearer and they were always a delight, so intent, so concerned that it should be perfect.

Very fortunately Simmons had sustained only mild concussion and had been allowed out of the hospital into my uncle's care after only two days' observation. It was soon after his arrival that my uncle called, saying that Geoffrey wanted to see me. My uncle's demeanour had changed. He looked older.

His shoulders drooped. I found myself at Geoffrey's bedside late that evening.

'Crispin, dear boy – Geoffrey wanted to speak to you.' My uncle sat the other side of the bed, the two old friends glanced at one another. They had obviously come to some kind of decision.

'I had been concerned not to trouble you ...' He did not mention my illness. 'But things have happened, and I feel that you should be put into possession of all the facts. I am so sorry, dear boy, I should have spoken to you before. Geoffrey?'

The older man in the bed eyed me, his hands moved a little on the quilt. He still looked weary, with a heavy bandage over the left side of his forehead, but he was strong enough to talk.

'This was not the first accident in the Song School, Mr Crispin. You know now, I suppose, about Mr Jeremy?'

'Yes – I have gathered that he had an accident there too.' I paused, so much seemed to be shrouded in secrecy. 'Did he ... did he die?'

My uncle leaned forward – a serious face.

'Yes, he did, my boy. I hadn't wanted to worry you.' He looked away. I had the strangest feeling, almost as if he felt guilty about something. 'I had not wanted to worry you unduly. But Geoffrey here sees more to it than coincidence, and I am impelled' – he shook his head – 'I am impelled to agree.' He took a deep breath. 'Jeremy Sideons had been interested in those carvings too, which is why I had been disturbed at your interest. Geoffrey, do explain.' He sat back, quiet.

'Well, sir, it's like this. That story you told about the singing, Mr Jeremy told me something like it. At first when he arrived we got on particularly well. It was then that he told me about what he had seen, and about the inscription. He said it was written along the base of those carvings. It's what I wanted to show you. He gave me this.'

My uncle handed me a piece of paper with a Latin inscription on it.

Cum tandem perfecto munere ero liberatus, cum pueri duodeviginti aureo choro carmen tollent, cum luna plenis radiis e caelo fulgebit hominesque deos summo apparatu celebrabunt, tum demum adveniet quidam summo imperio praeditus qui auctoritatem dignitatemque meam ipse suscipiet. Tum mihi quidem aderit tempus redeundi, tum homines simplicis animi ad voluntatem meam iterum regam. Crispino

I translated it:

When at length with my task performed I will have been set free, when eighteen boys in a golden choir raise their song, when the moon with full rays shines from the heavens, and men worship the gods with full preparation, then at last will come a man endowed with power who will himself undertake my authority and dignity. Then for me will come the time of return, then men of simple mind will again rule to my will. Crispin ...

I looked up. 'Is that all there is?'
The old man shook his head.
'No, he was going to collect the rest of it. He asked me if I knew what it was about, but something seemed to come over him quite sudden like. One evening friendly and confiding and the next morning, well, he looked different – as if he hadn't slept – and I asked him if he had had a poor night and he quite jumped, snarling at me. I was quite took aback. He said it was none of my business what he did with his own time.'
My uncle interrupted.
'I hadn't known the young man before, but some time after this he came to see me, quite out of the blue, and asked for my help. He was in quite a state, poor chap, perspiration standing out on his forehead, and his hands shaking. He said he wanted to show me something, to get evidence he said, whilst there was still time. He said something about a harvest moon but I didn't understand it. And then he was dead. His accident must have happened about an hour or so before our proposed meeting. So whatever he was doing with that ladder in the Song School must have been pretty important to the context of the meeting.'

'The evidence you see ...' Geoffrey chimed in. 'That's why I wanted to help you look at those carvings, sir. I wanted to see the whole of that inscription myself.'

'And why I didn't want you to look, you understand?' my uncle concluded. 'What we've got ends with your name – Crispin. You seem in some way implicated.'

'Yes ...' I was puzzled. 'I see, or at least I begin to.'

'There's some link between the death of Jeremy Sideons and ...'

'The name Crispin,' I added, thoughtful. It had triggered the two memories, the one of the paper in Jeremy's pocket that had Jeremy Sideons written on it and the muffled shout I had heard when in my room. It needn't have been outside – it could have been from the peep-window in my wardrobe. It could have been Geoffrey's voice before his fall.

I told them of both things, but like most people suffering from concussion the elderly man couldn't remember what had happened. All he could recall was climbing the ladder and finding something, something which even now troubled him.

But the consequences of the voice being his were obvious. The boys – or some of them at least – were responsible for his accident, and so too possibly responsible for killing a man.

'You see, Crispin, there's more to this than meets the eye.' Again the two older men glanced at one another, and there again I detected something in the glance. I couldn't quite describe it, shame perhaps; that was it – they looked ashamed.

'Some years ago, when you were still at school, there was an occurrence here, at the cathedral. One Christmastime, I won't trouble you with the details, but I've never really forgiven myself. It involved something more than the natural order of things, and I am very much afraid it might have something to do with that inscription.'

Geoffrey made a move as if to comfort him, but he continued:

'The details don't matter now but I am a man of God, Crispin, and if something is wrong and perhaps very wrong and those young people are involved, as what you saw seemed to indicate ... if they are involved in some kind of evil, we must do all we can to protect them.'

He looked at his old colleague.

'We need to investigate.' He stood up, apparently ready for action.

'What now? But, Uncle, it's late.' I looked at my watch.

But he was definite, decisive.

'I won't shirk my duty again. And your name appears on the inscription. It may be a coincidence, but I fear that it isn't. We will investigate now.'

They were not definite about what it was they feared – but fear it certainly was. I was sure they knew more than they told, or at least they suspected a particular thing of which they didn't speak – but I wouldn't ask. They had their reasons for not making it plain, and I knew it wasn't mistrust of me. Somehow I felt better than I had in a long time.

*

My uncle and I left the house, after severe words from my uncle to his friend.

'On no account invite anyone in, however well you know them or however innocent they may be. And if anything comes through the letter box, a slip of paper, a note, leave it alone. You simply mustn't touch it, even if it is addressed to you – don't accept it.'

It seem an astonishingly elaborate set of instructions. I found the phrase 'accept it' particularly odd, but again I trusted him. Geoffrey had his own work to do. Several ancient tomes lay on the bed; he was to be concerned with looking something up.

The clock was striking the hour as we left the house. Eleven o'clock. It was a starlit night and a large moon hovered high above the mass of the tower that stood out against the stars, silent and immense.

'It will soon be full moon,' I said in a conversational way.

'Yes it will,' said my uncle but the tone was one of portent.

The Song School was silent and dark; the door creaked a little as we entered. I was aware of the ringing sound of our shoes echoing into the recesses.

The porter had told me that the choir boys had offered to

take the ladder away for him, but he had been grumpy and thought ill of the offer and so it was still lying against the side.

My uncle turned to me and whispered.

'We can't use the lights; some of the dormitory windows overlook this part of the buildings. We don't want to attract attention. I have a flashlight with me.' He extracted a large torch from his great coat pocket. We manhandled the long ladder to the vertical and lowered it gently aginst the wall to the first figure of the series. It scraped on the stonework. I took the torch from him and climbed the ladder in the dark. We had decided to use the light only for my work and I was glad; it was quite a height, and in the darkness I could not be aware of how far I was from the marble pavement. My uncle leant against the foot of the ladder, his shoe wedged against the last rung.

The torch was held under my arm as I inspected the carving. The inscription was there, but I could only make out a few words at a time. I would have to move the ladder all the way along before being able to copy out the whole thing. The figures were bigger than they looked from the ground. The ladder only extended to the plinth on which they stood and they were about a quarter life size so I had to lean up against them to see properly.

They were indeed beautifully done. The folds of the Abbot's flowing gown were intricately carved, the cowl hanging over his head. I touched the hood. It looked delicate enough to give under my hands, but it was cold and hard, in fact very cold; it transmitted its cold to me, to my fingers, my arm – right to the elbow – tingled with the cold.

I was inquisitive – my fingers stroked the stone effigy, the workmanship was so good that it felt as if one could feel the shape of the head inside the cowl. My fingers extended around the contours of the hood. I knew from other cathedral carving I had seen that even if up high, like this particular example, or out of sight, the workmen often carved exactly what they wanted to portray. My fingers extended inside the hood. I wondered if there would be a face. In all probability no one had been this close to the sculptures for centuries, possibly since the last sculpture had put down the last chisel used to carve the work. It had never been cleaned. One could see that from the darkness of the figures against the otherwise light coloured stonework of the wall. I was probably the first to touch the inside of the hood since the mason had last taken his chisel away.

What my fingers met first puzzled me and then the realisation made me jerk my hand away nearly losing the torch. I clung back to the ladder.

'Are you all right?' My uncle's call was alarmed at the sudden movement that rocked the ladder.

'Yes ... Yes, I think so,' I whispered, harsh in the dark.

I recovered from the initial shock. I shone the torchlight full on the carving but it hadn't moved, and I couldn't get the light far enough round the enclosing arch to penetrate the blackness under cover of the hood.

I steeled myself. This is what we had come to discover – it was necessary.

My fingers again extended inside the hood but this time there was no sudden feeling of warmth. There was no hot breath from deep inside the cowl – but the features were there. I felt them, the long muzzle, the teeth bared, as if in a kind of snarl.

I felt suddenly very vulnerable. The wind had got up outside the windows and I could hear it pressing against the ancient leaded lights, the scraping of trees or foliage too, blown against the glass.

I shone the torchlight down to the side of the figure. I wanted to see the sheepdog, or what I had imagined to be a dog. I shone the light about. It surely had been here. I remembered it plainly, although I couldn't see it clearly from ground level. But the stone drapery fell clear and straight to the plinth on which the statue stood. It was like my illness again. I was sure of things – and yet uncertain. But this time I had evidence, I knew I had it recorded on my sketch pad. It had looked like a long-legged dog, standing as if mostly hidden behind the folds of the Abbot's cloak.

The next figure was too far over. I had to descend the ladder again and move across. I spoke to my uncle of the discovery, and he was non-committal in the darkness. I would dearly have loved to look at his face, to sense if he believed me or not, but I climbed again to inspect the next figure.

It was in a monk's habit – with trepidation I extended my fingers inside the covering hood and this time found another form. It was almost a skull, the remains of flesh I could feel cold and stretched over the bone, the deep hollow holes of the eyes, its scalp still sparsely covered by the remains of a sparse hair line. The garment had been sculptured to appear slightly open, and the hand that held it open I saw in the torchlight, skeletal and talloned, a fierce-looking hand of the long dead.

I climbed down the ladder shaken. This wasn't the work for one such as I, in the depths of the night. The next was the shepherd. I felt actual relief to peer at the face – so much the human face of medieval man, his staff held in a rough, calloused hand. There was something in the features that struck a cord – almost like recognition – but the old medieval face with its distant medieval style defied my wondering.

The first of the sheep too was quite normal – the carved stone wool looked soft enough to bury one's hands in, its fat hide full and well fed.

The next I noticed seemed less well fed. It was more an intimation of difference than a difference in its physical proportions, but it appeared somehow slightly narrower limbed, the wool hanging on a less full body.

The next again was distinctly different when one got close to it – the head altered in some way, its mouth open as if in a plaintive bleating.

The next, different again, its mouth wider open, with what looked like a wide tongue protruding.

I noticed that the next seemed to stand higher – with longer legs – a distinctly narrower body, yet covered still with a full fleece. But to the touch one could tell a transformation had manifested itself inside the covering coat of wool; its mouth too was open, wider than its previous neighbour, with the wedge-shaped protruberance from inside. It stood above the words:

'*When the moon with full rays …*' It was about a full moon.

*

As I moved along the line I recognised the signs, the slow, but steady transformation, the heads slightly further back, standing a little higher and more emaciated under the covering fleece, and the inscription below the figures become fuller each time – a prophecy. There were eighteen in all before I reached the dark corner with the final figure that had eluded my sketching a week or two earlier, almost out of sight in the dark recess.

By the last of the flock it was apparent that under the fleece there was in fact not a sheep at all. The open mouth, easily mistaken for bleating, had with it – I knew before I put my fingers in, another mouth – a long sharp muzzle with teeth protruding.

I had descended and was about to help my uncle move the ladder to inspect the last strange figure when he stopped me with an abrupt movement of his hand.

His voice came harsh in the darkness.

'Do you hear something?'

I listened, but could only hear the wind that had been pressing against the windows all through the time of our work.

'No, I don't.' But then I did. It was some way off – chanting – it was coming from the direction of the school passageway by which we had entered.

He moved quickly for an old man.

'Help me put the ladder down. We must be away.'

We edged the ladder down and back to its original position. He led the way towards the other end of the Song School, struggling with his keys.

'Shine the light here.'

I shone the torch on his keyring as he sorted through them, selecting a small old key. He pushed his way to the back of one of the carved stalls.

'This is the old entrance into the cathedral. It's not used now.' The lock clicked and the small wooden door opened silently.

We passed out onto a stone staircase that led downwards. He closed the door behind him, leaning against it breathing heavily.

'All this excitement's too much for an old man!'

I didn't have to see his face to know that he spoke with his characteristic smile.

'They're on time, you see.' He pulled out his Hunter watch and shone the torch on it. 'Twelve-thirty when all Christian men ought to be abed.' He at least didn't sound as anxious as his quick commands and movement had just displayed. I wondered if perhaps it was relief, but then again he did seem to enjoy excitement.

He listened at the door. The chanting could now be heard through the heavy oak. We had made our getaway just in time.

*

Our journey down the flight of stone steps and through the great darkened north transept of the cathedral would have frightened me had I been in the company of anyone else but my uncle. Either because of his long acquaintance with the building or because of some inner strength he seemed not at all perturbed, so I gained confidence from him.

'We must away to your room now, I'm afraid, young fellow. We haven't finished our night's escapade yet.'

I made a noise which I hoped sounded like agreement but I wanted no more of it that night.

He touched my arm gently, recognising my apprehension.

'You've done very well – very well indeed. We must get that inscription deciphered. My Medieval Latin isn't as good as yours and we must get a sight of what they're up to.'

The chanting could easily be heard when we got into my rooms. My uncle moved about quietly, taking the clothes from the racks and placing them on the bed in the darkness.

'You sit there,' he whispered.

'I'll watch.'

I was glad to sit down on the bed. I could see his face illuminated by the palest of candlelight coming through the peep window. He perched on a stool, his bushy white eyebrows working as he studied what went on below.

The chanting rose and fell and suddenly there was silence. He quickly backed away. The sudden movement arrested me. There was another glow – a different kind of light – which seemed for an instant to brighten the room. Not from the peep window but from the walls.

I looked at my watch almost by reflex action – it was ten minutes past one.

I felt an extraordinary sensation in the top of my head, a kind of tugging. I held my head. He was looking at me intently, and then the chanting began again.

He leant over and motioned me to the peep. I looked out – there they were again as I had seen them before, with the robes and hoods up, I counted them, eighteen – eighteen of them, the whole boys' choir. Or was it? The choirboys stood around the edge of the same chalked circle with its symbols, but I thought I saw another cowled figure in the candlelight taller than the boys at the further edge in the gloom. And the chalked symbols were different. There was another marking, like a triangle; the figure I thought I could discern was standing away from me, at the triangle's base. The apex, the point of the triangle, pointed in our direction. It could have been a triangle but, I realised, it could equally have been a pointer-arm, an arrow, pointing in my direction.

They began to move, holding their candles they began to move round the outer rim, chanting. I caught some of the words. I noticed my uncle feeling in his jacket. Extracting a pen he began to scribble on the back of an envelope.

It was like a dance. They moved around the aisle – the circle the eighteen of them – but the other taller figure I could just discern didn't move, and I realised, watching them, that they moved as it were through the figure. It appeared to stand motionless, not carrying a candle and each of the smaller figures moved through that dark shape as if it were not there, their outline very slightly sharper, with a pale light as they moved through the form. I watched as each of the figures passed through. Their candles became dim as they passed through the shadowy figure and yet they were somehow illuminated, and then as the last of the eighteen passed through the shadowy figure all was darkness. I was looking out into darkness. A cold breeze blew through the opening and I shivered. There was no sound. It was as if the Song School was empty and deserted, and had been for hours.

My uncle didn't move, and when I turned to speak to him he quickly placed a finger over my mouth – a warm, living finger. It was a comfortingly human gesture. He tugged at my sleeve, and I followed him out of the room into my small sitting room. He closed the door quietly behind him.

'I think you can turn the lamp on now.'

I did, with relief but the brightness of the light was painful to the eyes after the hours of gloom.

'I think you need a cup of tea, or do you young fellows only have coffee nowadays?'

He boiled the kettle that sat on the floor by my desk and busied himself making two mugs of coffee.

He searched around looking for milk.

'I'm afraid I've only got powdered.' His brows came together as he unscrewed the jar of powdered milk and ladled it into the mugs.

'Tut tut, dear boy, tut tut. What remarkably uncivilized habits you do have ...'

He handed me the mug. He looked into his own mug of steaming liquid, and his lips compressed, shaking his head a little.

'Well, my boy, there we have it.' He looked up, bringing himself back to the matter of our nocturnal wanderings.

'You've done very well – very well. I'm sorry you're involved.' He shrugged his large shoulders. 'But we can't choose these things. Come, drink this apology for coffee and I'll take you back to Canons Walk. You can't stay here – that much is plain, and we need to look at what we have got of the inscription and see how Geoffrey is. If I'm not much mistaken he will have had a visitor tonight.'

I held the mug in both hands – confused. But I was somehow comforted by my uncle's strength of purpose. He was no longer the demoralised elderly man I had seen earlier.

'Do you know what is going on, Uncle?'

He looked at me full and hard.

'I'm very much afraid I do, my boy. I had thought it was all over – but it isn't. I'll explain better when we get home.' He looked into his mug with undisguised disdain at the instant coffee.

'And I think I'll get you a decent glass of brandy – to wash this stuff out of your system.' He grinned. 'You've earned it. Oh, and bring those sketches of yours, we will be needing them.'

The cathedral clock sounded in the distance – chiming the hour – it struck a resonant one. I looked at my watch.

I repeated the information, the hands standing at one o'clock.

'But it can't be …' I looked up at him puzzling. He pulled at his lower lip with his thumb and forefinger.

'I know,' he said.

*

We got back to the house and found Geoffrey up and waiting for us, one of the old books under his arm. As we opened the front door he came into the hall.

'You were right, Canon. Something did come.' He pointed to a scrap of thick yellow paper on the floor. 'But I heeded what you said and haven't touched it even though it was addressed to me. I found something of interest in here too.' He tapped the book with his forefinger.

My uncle struggled to get out of his greatcoat.

'Good. Now we will see what they're made of.' He leant over to pick up the paper and he straightened again, looking thoughtful. 'No, no, it would be better I think if you did it, Crispin – just pick it up for me, could you, my boy?'

I was certainly puzzled by this behaviour, but had learnt to obey his whims. I stooped to pick it up, as my hands closed around it the lights appeared to dim in the hall. I could see the faces of Geoffrey and my uncle, but a dark mist seemed to stand between me and them and then the cold assailed me – and the faint vibration on the edge of sound which seemed to tremble my hand and arm, reaching up inside me. It was a chanting that passed on its way and diminished again. The lights appeared to glow again, the warmth returned.

My uncle helped me to a seat by the umbrella stand.

He looked at me carefully, as a doctor might look for symptoms in the eyes of a patient.

'Is that better now – have you recovered?'

'Yes, I think so … But what was it?' I shook my head regaining complete control. 'It was … it was like …'

'The occasion before, when you discovered that piece of paper in Jeremy's suit pocket. Yes, yes, I expected something like that. I'm sorry to have used you, my boy, but I knew that you were sensitive to these things. You have the gift –' He looked at Geoffrey – 'as it was foretold,' and then back to me. 'It might not have been so obvious if I had tried it and we have to know. Can you stand?'

'Yes – yes I'm better now.'

'Right – you've certainly deserved your drink – or would you like some whisky in hot milk?'

'No, thank you, Uncle – I'll take the brandy!'

We went into the sitting room and sat in the deep comfortable old armchairs – I was still holding the paper. It had Geoffrey's name on it. I began to unfold it. It was in the same childish hand but it was a note in English – a simple message, expressing hopes for his full recovery and saying how awful it was to have another accident in the Song School, the floors being so slippery. It was unsigned.

My uncle came back into the room. I was just about to hand the note to Geoffrey.

'*No!*' He nearly dropped the tray. 'Good heavens, no. You mustn't touch, it, Geoffrey. Don't even look at it.'

We had both started back.

'Sorry, Uncle. I was forgetting. But whatever is it all about – why can't Geoffrey have the note?'

'Because it's intended for him. Remember the effects both notes have had on you? They're not simply pieces of paper. They carry something far more than just the writing on them. Give it to me. Things aren't always what they seem. Geoffrey

would have let himself in for more than he bargained for had
he accepted this.'

He took it and placed it carefully on a table set before the
fire. He placed a glass tumbler over it.

'We don't want this getting lost, do we?'

He handed me my drink and one to Geoffrey.

'I'm sure this won't do you any harm, Geoffrey!' He picked
one up for himself. 'To success, Gentlemen.'

'To success,' we both repeated, not really understanding
what kind of success we toasted.

My uncle was animated; he fussed over the burning coals in
the fire and then settled himself in his armchair his drink in his
hand. He looked full at the elderly verger.

'I think now we have gathered sufficient evidence to begin to
put the puzzle together.'

He fumbled in his pocket and drew out the folded envelope
and put it on the table beside the upturned glass.

'I'm afraid I didn't get much here. Latin verses ...
translated, if I'm right,' he said frowning at the envelope.

'Come out of him, spirit with the gift ...' He paused. 'Gift ...
is that right?'

I looked at him.

'Not really – it's more like "sight" or "power".'

'And then it repeats. "Come out and join us in our dance"
or something like that.' He grunted. 'We need more than that
– we must have it all. It is obviously some kind of "calling up".
But of whom? For what purpose? Suppose we look at that
inscription of yours?'

I extracted the notes from my pocket and flattened them on
the table before the fire.

'Do draw your chairs up – I want to explore what we've got.
Geoffrey – put the book on the table.'

We sat around the small table looking at the items of
'evidence' as my uncle described them.

'Let us look at the facts as we have them, ignoring the past,
Geoffrey. Just what we have as experience this time.'

He wrote them down, and placed them together – neatly –

like an expert putting a complicated jigsaw together. Each individual experience could easily have been discounted, or at least thought only a curiosity, but together ... He detailed a possible pattern, which would have been laughable were it not for the man who made the assessment.

The carving was, he believed, a kind of code. The mason who chiselled it with such care was chronicling something, but I was really uncertain as to whether it was in the past or the future; and my uncle still seemed to be reserved about telling us all. The Abbot. (There was obviously more to the Abbot than my uncle thought appropriate to say in his factual analysis.) The Abbot led the procession, yet he was not a man. Outwardly a leader of his flock, inwardly something quite different.

The next figure extends the theme – the Abbot's power is followed by – or included – death – perhaps power over death, or perhaps his power extending beyond death.

Then the simple shepherd – a real flesh and blood man, trusting, following the figures he believes he recognises, the outward vestures of whom he respects, unaware of what lies inside the robes.

The sheep follow – eighteen of them. My uncle pointed out that the number was significant. There have always been eighteen choir boys – from the earliest statutes, when the choir was first formed under the patronage of Abbot Benedict in the fourteenth century. Eighteen unblemished virgin boys – it was quite specific in detailing that.

And the sheep change, one by one in a chain of transformation, into what? Perhaps wolves in sheeps' clothing?

I couldn't help smiling at the idea.

And finally the shadowy figure we hadn't been able to examine; standing above the inscription we hadn't been able to copy down, walking on two legs – but with a snout – just visible, just coming onto the scene, following the procession. What did he represent? Something in time with the rest, something in the fourteenth century or something which was a result of all that went before? Something out of time or perhaps in the future or perhaps in our time?

I sat enthralled, my drink untouched, but the elderly verger only nodded. He had had his own inklings of what these things portended, but was silent.

'And what of time?' My uncle looked at me. He held his finger up to emphasise the point. 'Not once, but twice you have mentioned time. Apparently out of sequence, a sort of brief dislocation – just a few minutes. But as you said yourself – it can't be.'

He paused for some minutes, watching me assimilate the idea.

'The chanting has something to do with that. The ritual we have both observed. You know when I backed away from the peep window – I thought they had seen me. Quite suddenly they stopped and all looked in our direction, holding the candles up to us. But they hadn't seen us – I don't think they had seen anything. Before I backed away I caught sight of their faces in the candlelight. They all had their eyes shut.'

I was amazed by this but wanted to know his deduction.

'It was about then that you felt something. You put your head in your hands. What was it?'

'I don't know really. I saw a glow – brightness of some kind – and then a feeling in my head – on top of my head.' I put my hand up. He moved forward placing his fingers on the top of my skull.

'What, there?'

He touched the point exactly.

'Yes, right there, like a tugging feeling – as if I had a hook there pulling upwards.'

He settled back in his armchair and nodded. His fingertips together touching his lips – his white shaggy eyebrows drew close together.

'Yes, that is the fontanel, the last part of the skull to knit together when you are a child, an "innocent". It's that place from which the spirit is supposed to emerge in spirit travel. You were being called out of your body.'

This was all becoming more and more incredible – but yet I

went on with it, asking a question as if we were talking about something quite normal.

'And the slips of paper bearing messages?'

He lifted the tumbler carefully, keeping his thumb on the scrap of yellow parchment.

'Yes ...' He held it up to the light of the fire.

'If we aren't too careful with you, you little messenger ...' He turned it over and examined the other side. 'You will get lost, won't you? Just like the other one did.'

He looked across at me.

'No, it wasn't your fault the other one went missing. It had done its job. It must have escaped through your window or into your electric fire perhaps.'

'What do you mean?'

He carefully put the paper back under the tumbler and made sure the glass completely covered it.

'If I'm not too mistaken, when we have some more time – and can examine it properly – we will find it contains something else. Your reactions to the slip you found in Jeremy Sideon's pocket gave me the clue. You see, the choirboys weren't here when Jeremy had his so-called accident. In fact, no one was about at all. He wasn't pushed by any human hand, you mark my words, it was something else. I would surmise that he had realised something of what was going on. He knew he was in great danger. He had been singled out for some purpose – his reaction to Geoffrey seems to indicate that, but then he came to me. Goodness knows why he chose me. But he did and he was found out. He was a kind of forerunner. He was expendable. And now Jeremy's out of the way they have got what they wanted.' He looked at me, I shuddered. It was all too obvious ...

He continued.

'It's contained in the paper I expect – a kind of psychic message. You felt the darkness and cold. I watched you when you touched it – you have the gift. But the message wasn't for you – yet you felt the power. If it had been intended for you I don't expect you would be here now.'

I looked into his eyes. They were serious and wise. I could do nothing but believe him. I looked at the apparently innocent piece of parchment pinned to the table by its glass.

'That's why I couldn't let Geoffrey touch it.' He stopped and corrected himself. 'Whatever it is we are up against will use every device it can – including your accidental offering of it to Geoffrey just now. We all have to be very careful, especially if we ...' the pause and correction again ... 'especially if it knows we are getting close to the truth which it might well ... I don't know how powerful it is. And we don't know all there is to know yet. We must proceed with the utmost caution. It will use any weakness, any slight non-attention to detail, anything at all."

I was aware of his eyes, serious and penetrating. What he said had force. No longer the gentle amicable old cleric; he spoke with an air of authority that made me shudder.

'Come.' He settled back in his chair.

'Drink your drink and we will hear what Geoffrey has to tell us. It's a long night.'

As he spoke the hall clock chimed the three quarters – and was echoed by the booming of the distant cathedral clock. It was a quarter to three in the morning; a burning coal dropped from the fire basket, scattering ashes on the grate.

The elderly verger leant forward taking up the book he had been carrying when we arrived back.

'I think your remark the other day about Red Riding Hood had more in it than you thought, Mr Crispin.'

I thought back over our discussions. It was hardly funny, but like my uncle the old verger seemed to find room in the incredible business for one occasional smile.

'Well, Canon, I found what you were looking for.' He turned to the front page of the crumbling old book.

He coughed and read the title: '*Daemoniacs and Folklore – an enquiry into the evidence for Demons – an Hypothesis of the Rev. Mr Farmer.*'

He looked up.

'What does MDCCLXXIX mean, Canon? I always forget my

Roman numbers?' My uncle calculated on his fingers and at last answered '1779'.

Geoffrey craned his neck, and fingered through the old pages until he came to his book mark.

'Here it is: "Lyttle Red Riding Hood. The tale comes to us from Europe ... of Germanic origin in the forest region known as The Black Forest ..." Just a moment, it's further on ... ah, yes, here it is. "Speculation can abound as to whether the Grandmother really was eaten by the wolf. Why did not the little girl immediately perceive that it was a wolf and not indeed her grandmother. Grandmother, what big eyes you have – Grandmother, what long ears you have – Grandmother, what sharp teeth you have, seem to indicate the little girl's examination of her actual Grandmother. Is it not more likely that the tale is coded, the truth being too horrifying – that her Grandmother was indeed turning into a wolf and that she could see both human and canine features together ..."

'And then it goes on: "The ending of the story with the axeman extracting the old woman from inside the wolf seems to be an addition to the story." It then says something about the evidence in other folklore for werewolves and that there has never been an English equivalent, presuming that the stories – and the base in historical fact – are apparently endemic to Eastern Europe.'

He looked up, the book lying open in his lap.

'And that is it – all I could find.'

My uncle nodded.

'Well, it is an idea ...' He frowned, pulling at his lower lip with thumb and forefinger. 'We can, I think, do little more now, but keep vigilant. You are the one nearest to them, my boy. The responsibility will devolve mainly upon you. Make sure you keep us in touch with what develops. I think you, Geoffrey, had better keep in the background – stay here for a while, I think. They know you are inquisitive and they have tried to get rid of you in a pretty straightforward way – and now this.' He nodded at the slip of parchment. 'A more sophisticated way. I think it would be best if you stay out of sight.'

He looked up from gazing at the parchment.

'Of course this is a weakness.' He leaned over and examined it. 'They need something material, something physical to make contact. It's in the paper.' He looked up at us in turn. 'It has to be communicated by physical touch.' He looked down at it again tapping the rim of the glass. 'A weakness. It's the only one. You have to accept it – like a transaction – like a … covenant – that's what the Hebrews called it. It has to be accepted and agreed to by physical contact – by your wanting it – like to read this, you see, to take it up and read. It's a matter of free choice, as inviting someone into the house.' His eyes lit up with excitement. 'And he can't overcome that. He can't force anyone against their will.'

He found this so called 'weakness' such an important matter that he forgot to correct himself in talking in that curious singular style again. It seemed as if he felt we weren't dealing with a group – but rather with one individual.

'I've never been convinced about Werewolves, but maybe I should change my mind.'

*

I awoke the next morning, having slept well. At first I was disconcerted to find myself at my uncle's house, in a bedroom I used as a child visitor. Then it came back to me, not as a sharp well defined memory but somehow rather blurred. I realised later that that curious effect was all part of my ensnarement, but I didn't know that at the time. Indeed it worked perfectly, because, like the memory of night fears and fantasies, the daylight in a great part dispersed my seriousness on the subject. Even they had been able to smile about it in their funny elderly style of humour …

To be perfectly honest, another dream was more central to my mind as I awoke. It was one I had had before and concerned Rupert, the head choirboy. Actually I felt rather embarrassed at meeting my uncle and the elderly verger over breakfast, as one might after an occasion of some misdemeanour, where one had to face those who had witnessed one's indiscretion.

But fortunately they too seemed bent on making little of the night's happenings.   My uncle civilly hoped I had had a good night and I assured him that I had slept very soundly. The elderly verger sat at the breakfast table rather like the dormouse at the Mad Hatter's Tea Party – somnolent and docile.

I had to be away quickly, and soon found myself immersed in the hour by hour routine of the school which I much enjoyed. The whole series of episodes of the night before became, when I did think of them, increasingly embarrassing; somehow the unreality of it against life in a daylit crowded school was incongruous – grotesque and false.

In our discussions of the previous evening I had not counted on extra Medieval Latin which occupied an hour of my afternoon and involved teaching a group consisting entirely of senior choirboys. The foolishness of my uncle's warning against accepting pieces of paper from the choirboys was now too obvious. I could just imagine Mr Fitzpatrick, the head of classics, accepting Demonology as an excuse for not taking in prep to mark.

They were, as usual, attentive and friendly.

Rupert particularly seemed to want to please, and I was aware of the danger of showing my preference too obviously.

On two occasions after setting an exercise I looked up to find him gazing at me, and when I looked up he would smile.

On both occasions I felt the same glow of pleasure, but commented that he ought to get on. And on both occasions he said he had finished, and he had. He brought his work to me, standing I felt, rather too close to me as I marked the work, and it was all complete, and beautifully done. He had even corrected an error I had made in my typed hand-out, which was quite incredible, as if he were practised in using Medieval Latin daily.

After the lesson the rest of the group left the room but he lingered saying he wanted to speak to me. He said he wondered if he could have some extra tuition, showing me a piece of work he had been doing.

It was a piece of illuminated manuscript work which was truly beautiful. I said so and he smiled with pride. I was apprehensive for a fleeting moment as I held the page. It was thick vellum, but of course it would be if it was properly to conform to the character of illuminated script, and I felt no ill effects at its touch – quite the opposite in fact, apart from suddenly being aware what a foolish old man my uncle was. I seemed, as I held the sheet, to be aware of things in a different way, to somehow gain a little confidence; it occurred to me for the first time how attainable my secret desires were, it was merely a matter of taking what I wanted. There was no reason for extra tuition but I said that certainly he could come to my rooms sometimes and we would go over the work together.

He left his extra work with me and went on his way, pausing at the door to glance back with those strange eyes.

When he'd gone I experienced a conflict within me, a whole range of conflicting emotions, desires and warnings, but the majority of the warnings – at least of my uncle's kind – were ridiculous, the rambling of a man too old. There could be nothing sinister in the open affection of a young boy. It may be wrong to get emotionally involved with one's pupils – but it wasn't the kind of wrong my uncle's concerns voiced.

And anyway, I told myself I had been commissioned to investigate – to get close to them and my uncle was the Precentor. A small voice inside my head seemed to say your uncle is the Precentor ... and if anyone questioned a boy being in my rooms then I could refer them to my uncle's injunction ... to get to know them.

For the first time since my illness I felt in control of the situation – I knew what I wanted and there was ample excuse. I was warmed by the feeling; strangely light-headed – and pleased – I felt I had purpose again.

I saw my uncle only briefly before evensong. He had a chapter meeting to attend, the final arrangements for the great 700th Anniversary Service the next day. The choir had been practising some specially commissioned anthems since mid-October, and there was much excitement about the impending festival.

One anthem was particularly beautiful, a modern work in Latin with a great orchestral accompaniment entitled 'The Shepherd's Song' with several parts. It was to celebrate the beginning of the building, with a solo part for the Abbot who commissioned the building and one for a shepherd who represented the wealth of the monastic lands. Rupert had been practising the treble part of the Shepherd Boy.

I found it hard to meet my uncle's eyes as he spoke. He asked if I was all right, and I rather snapped back that of course I was and apologised. Lack of sleep, I said, had shortened my temper. He said he wouldn't be in at Evensong – he wanted to make sure Geoffrey was quite well – but if I didn't mind he would come to my rooms at midnight. He wanted to get a proper recording of the chant – it was the words he wanted.

I said I would be waiting for him.

During Evensong my eyes wandered over to where Rupert stood – he looked ethereal in the light of the choir stall lamps, for the evenings were quite dark now. I also noticed another figure behind the choir on the opposite side to me, sitting back in the shadow of a canopied stall. There were still a number of visitors at the service, although autumn was well advanced, but this one figure struck a cord somewhere. It looked like a monk in a brown habit, but I couldn't see him clearly. When everyone stood for the psalm I expected him to stand too, but he stayed seated in the shadows.

After the service I was delayed by an astonishing interview with the choirmaster. He asked if I would take over the solo part of the Abbot in the anthem. The tenor soloist had suddenly been taken ill and I was the only person thought capable of learning the Latin part and doing justice to the music by the next day. It was a great honour – and I walked from the choir stalls in a daze of pleasure and apprehension, a wonderful feeling, everything suddenly seemed to be going right for me.

When I came down the steps into the nave I saw the figure of the monk again. For anyone who knows Woolminster I do not have to explain the abysmal lighting in the nave; the lights, such as they are are too small, and hanging high up. It is a gloomy place in the dark evenings of autumn, but I instantly saw the figure, because he was talking to Rupert, who still wore his choir robes. It was very unusual indeed for a member of the choir to break from the procession, and I thought I'd use that as an excuse to go and talk with him. But as I approached they stopped talking and the hooded figure lay a hand on Rupert's head, in a kind of blessing, and walked away into the gloom at the west end of the building. I was more interested in the boy than the visitor and accosted him as he came back towards the north door.

'Hello, Rupert, what are you doing still here?'
He smiled his radiant smile.
'Oh, that was my godfather. He came to listen to us sing.'
'He's a monk?'
'Yes, he is,' he said.
I smiled back at him.
'Oh, that's interesting,' I said, my mind full of the news I had just received.

I had a curious sensation as we walked that he expected me to ask something else but I didn't and he seemed somehow relieved. I didn't know what gave me the impression. Perhaps he relaxed a little or something, but I wasn't really interested. It was just a good feeling to be talking with him and to know that I had been considered good enough to step in and take the part of the Abbot.

I sat up late that night, trying to learn the new part and waiting for my uncle. But I couldn't concentrate. I felt restless. The idea of spying on the boys troubled me. It was obviously all a series of random happenings; they didn't mean anything. My uncle had been able to spin them into a convincing tale last night, but now I felt so different about it. With Rupert on my mind – with conflicting loyalties – I found it hard to believe. An idea began to form itself in my mind when I heard the bedtime bell ringing and soon, for a whole random series of complex reasons I was convinced it was a good idea. When my

uncle arrived at just before midnight I made my excuses and
left him saying I was just going to the lavatory, and would be
back in a few moments. It took no time to be outside the senior
choristers' dormitory and I waited, concealed on the steps
leading to the next floor.

Nothing stirred. I heard the bell strike half past midnight,
and then the three quarter hour, still nothing happened. I
waited until the hour was striking. The resonant *one* was
vibrating in the dstance as I slipped into the dormitory.

The light of the near full moon shone through the
uncurtained windows and I was amazed how cold the room
was, not naturally cold – it was like walking into a freezer
room. But they were all there. I crept around the beds, to
where Rupert lay. They looked like ancient knights on their
tombs. There was not a sound, and their faces, like stone
carved effigies, lay face up, still as death. Each one, I noticed,
had his hands across his chest. A curious sensation stole over
me, as if I were in a crypt, and alone with the dead effigies of
the past. I told myself I was just being fanciful – they were only
boys sleeping ... peacefully. I crept out again.

My uncle was in a state of some agitation when I got back to
my rooms, both to know where I was and to tell of what he had
seen. When I explained he listened with a strange expression
on his face and then made me repeat what I had seen.

'But they have been down there. They came in at half past –
and stayed, chanting, I have the chant recorded.' He tapped a
small cassette recorder he had under his coat. 'But that isn't all.
The ouija game you mentioned – it happened again, and it
spelt out your name: Crispin.'

I was not prepared to listen further. It was true that I was
very tired, but also I had incontrovertible proof that what he
had seen or had imagined that he had seen was in some way
hallucinatory. People just couldn't be in two places at once.

I showed him to the door, explaining that I was too tired to
do any further analysis that night, that the next day was the
great Septuacentenary Service. I was ungracious, I realised
that, but I had to get my sleep. I hadn't told him about my

change of part – and was far too tired for social chatter.

He was obviously embarrassed about his final few words and the gift that he pressed upon me, but he gave me a pendant to wear round my neck. He apologised – and said that it was probably the foolishness of an old man – but that I should wear it at all times. He actually put it round my neck and it felt uncomfortable.

As soon as he had gone I did go to bed and was, in truth, asleep soon afterwards. But the dreams I had disturbed me. Again and again as I awoke and slept again the same recurring images troubles me: Rupert, his face distorted somehow, round and protruding, was calling me on, and the rest of the choir standing behind him. I followed him and the choir parting before me came to stand before a figure dressed as a monk, who was offering me something – something incandescent, spherical, in his hands. But his hands were cracked and taloned, the flesh peeling off them.

And I wanted the thing he held, but as I stepped forward I knew I had to offer him something in return, something from inside me. But I couldn't find in my mind what it was and as I went forward a choking sensation – a strangling feeling around my neck stopped me and he backed away.

I awoke with a terrible yearning, I wanted to know what it was I was to give him, I wanted the thing he offered me. I lay awake. I could feel the perspiration on my face. I so wanted to return to the dream – and receive the gift. I heard the cathedral clock striking the hour; it was five in the morning. I was almost in panic that I wouldn't get to sleep again and if I didn't sleep again I wouldn't receive the gift. The chain around my neck was cutting into the skin – it had got twisted somehow. I took it off and threw it to the end of the bed and at once felt better, ready for sleep, ready to receive the gift in the dream.

I slept again, the dream returned, but this time the boys' faces were beautiful and I was led towards the figure – again the figure held out the gift and I moved forward – the figure came towards me, no longer retreating and fearful of me. The hands that held the sphere were old, it was true, but not rotting and repulsive. They too held a beauty of their own and I knew what it was I had to give in exchange – a simple thing, so incredibly easy, so little in comparison to the gift. I knelt down before him extending my hands. It was just homage – so simple ... to worship ... so easy ...

But the dream was shattered. Fragments flew into a thousand pieces as I was dragged backwards and felt myself flying and pain in my head a sudden eruption to consciousness and the terrible noise. I awoke. Many things happened at once. I opened my eyes to see the creature above me – its four feet planted on the bed – its great salivating jaws open and red above my face, its snout sharp and the many-fanged mouth – its luminous eyes ablaze, and its breath hot on my face. I was paralysed but the thunderous banging on the door gave way to its crashing open and the figure of my uncle bundled in crying words, a torrent of words, ancient-sounding gutteral speech, a Hebrew tongue more ancient than Latin.

The sulphurous explosion over my chest cast noxious fumes through the room and fragmented dust smelling of age. My uncle collapsed at the foot of the bed.

I was still dazed when another figure appeared at the open doorway. It was Rupert, wearing a dressing gown.

'Sir, I heard a lot of noise ...'

I realised it was light. Looking at my bedside clock I saw it was quarter to seven. Surely it hadn't been light when my uncle entered the room?

'Is there anything I can do for you, sir. Are you all right, sir?' The question was not addressed to me but to my uncle. The boy was kneeling over the slumped figure of the old man.

I shook my head to clear it and staggered from the bed.

'Is he all right?' I had the strangest sensation of being somehow subordinate to the boy. He seemed to be in control somehow.

'I think the Canon's ill, sir. Could I perhaps get someone whilst you get him onto a chair?'

'Yes – yes of course – do go ...'

I struggled to get my uncle into the armchair. He was heavy, inert.

There would be a number of people about at this hour, and indeed there were. Very soon the Matron was with us.

I feebly explained that he had come early to deal with some things about the service but no one seemed interested in why my uncle should be about at such an early hour. The gaggle of masters directed by the Matron were soon taking him off to the Sanatorium. Matron seemed to think he had just fainted and would be better soon. My own mind was too confused for any logical thought. I merely kept repeating the silly phrase to myself 'two down, one to go' – it had no meaning.

'Can I do anything for you, sir?'

I looked up. Rupert stood just inside the doorway looking at me with his large blue eyes.

I sat down on the bed.

'No. I don't think so, thank you, Rupert. It's been a bit of a shock, everything happening at once.' He moved slightly further into the room.

'Yes ... I'm sure it has, sir, but you'll be feeling better soon – I know you will.' I looked up into his face. He smiled his smile. He had a curious air of confidence, and I found it hard to articulate it to myself. It was the right word – command – it was as if he were in command of the situation – and I, merely helpless.

But I did feel better – and I said so.

'I'm so glad, sir. If there is anything you want, just call for me – I'm here to help you, sir. We all are.' And then I became aware of the others – three other senior choristers standing silent in the doorway – but all of them wore that strange indulgent smile and their blue eyes watched me.

And I heard myself saying:

'Yes – I'll be all right now,' and Rupert replying:

'Yes, you'll be all right now. We will see you later, before the service. We have an appointment at six in the Cathedral.'

And I said we had – and knew that we had – before the great evening service celebrating the Seven Hundredth Anniversary of Abbot Benedict's building of the Minster.

They left me then and I still felt as if I were in some kind of dream, but not an unpleasant one, not like the state of semi-reality I had known in the depths of my illness, with the horrors lurking around every corner. This was rather a semi-dream state, when I was prepared to be organised, because – at some time – some unspecified time in the past – it had been pre-ordained that I should do this, and so there was no need for thought or decision-making; it was all in the hands of ... I wasn't quite sure, but I hadn't been sure when I was ill, so this was nothing startling. I could just relax, and wait for the evening.

My visions of the great hound assailed me only occasionally but I had become used to shutting out undesirable thoughts and I had much work to do to be ready for the evening. Only occasionally would I experience the fear – that there were so many things I didn't understand, that I was too involved in something I couldn't control, out of touch with the one man I could trust. But then my eyes would espy one of the choristers, with their great blue eyes, watching me, and I would be reassured, my fears somehow subsiding.

I learnt my new part during the day, the Abbot's part in the great first singing of 'The Shepherd's Song'. I spent the day with the organist and choirmaster – the choir were practising in the Song School. Others came and went, but I was always aware that one or two choirboys were in the vicinity – watching.

The cathedral was in a bustle, with the orchestra arriving and cables being laid for the sound transmission and the seating being arranged by the new head verger and his underlings.

The other canons fussed about worrying lest the Precentor should be indisposed for the whole day. They said he had recovered from his collapse but had gone home, but no-one could find him. The Dean scurried about making last minute preparations with the Bishop's chaplain. Several other important high officials were due to arrive and the bustle continued gathering momentum; but there – in a corner – or there in a stall, would be the choirboys, quiet, self possessed, somehow above the hurry and scurry, self-absorbed – but watchful, always watchful. I could feel their eyes upon me.

Lunchtime saw the arrival of the outside broadcast cameras. The organist and choirmaster, Edwin Lewis, was in a panic, concerned that he should look his best in the procession. The canons and other clerics bobbed and flustered, worried about their own parts; absorbed with how they would look, and whether all would be well. The new head verger becoming hysterical, lest the seating be re-arranged after all his careful planning and the whole huge building hummed with frantic preparations and worries.

But by late afternoon everything began to die away, near normality returned, although Evensong would not be sung tonight. As dusk fell the great building emptied and cameras and arc lights and cables and chairs were left unattended as all went their separate ways for the meals, and to greet the guests that had begun to flow into the town – great and low alike – to Palace and to Deanery, to School and the Woolmarket to the Mayor's Parlour and to the hotels they came, the largest throng to be seated in the building for living memory. And the building waited, emptied of all its people, silent; only pools of light, oases in the gloom of the nave and a few of the choir stall lights, throwing their yellow light over the patinaed stalls.

And I waited, standing there, alone, in the centre of the choir stalls, waiting facing the gloom in the west – then the sound, the light footfalls. They began to appear, from various directions, the red-hooded figures slowly gathering, without a word, they gathered around me, facing into the gloom, waiting. All was silence ...

The cathedral clock high above began to strike the hour, and in the gloom at the further end of the building a sudden crackle of electricity – a bright blue flash registered the fusing of some of the arc light cables and a movement caught in the electric flashes. A figure, silhouetted in the split second crackling, casting monstrous shadows against the walls of the cathedral. He was approaching from the west, he was coming to meet me – just as I had dreamt it – bearing his gift which was to cost so little. Just my agreement. Another blue white flash and an explosion of electricity hit the great interior. He was nearer, his power was immense. I could make out his figure as he moved slowly forward – dark – in a hood, moving towards me down the centre of the nave.

He began to mount the steps to the choir stalls. Soundless he moved toward me.

The last set of cables and lamps exploded into split-second life to die as suddenly, the shadows again etched like terrifying tortured talons against the ceiling. But I couldn't in that short space see under his cowl; his face was hidden.

The choir stood silent, not a muscle moving as he came towards us.

And suddenly there was a movement, a sound in the soundlessness of heavy feet – and a flitting figure.

'*Stop* – stop, I say!'

It was my uncle, another figure slightly behind his bulk. I felt a shock, a reaction, as if again awoken out of sleep. But the dark figure continued towards me and out of the folds of his mantle extended his hands bearing the gift.

'Stop!' my uncle's voice shouted.

'Crispen – listen to me.' His speed had brought him nearer than the dark figure. He clutched at my shoulder, a human touch, which was solid and hard and alive.

I could not tear my eyes away from the spectre that approached – only yards away. He held out the sphere, translucent and glowing with an inner light.

The old man was shaking me with his large hands.

'Crispen, I have the rest of the code. Don't touch him – don't accept – it's his only weakness, boy. He can't make you against your will. Crispen!' he shouted at me.

My eyes were fixed upon the spectre. The orb glowed in its hands ... the dark recesses of the cowl beckoned me to step towards him. From the corner of my eye I saw Geoffrey edging behind the figure.

'The end of the prophecy, boy – I have it. He's not offering you anything – it's all for him. There won't be anything of you left.'

I drew my eyes away from the spectre that stood before me and looked to my uncle.

'You have time, boy. Listen to me. Just a few moments – I beg you – just for a few moments ...'

Something of the spell seemed to break. There was no rush – the metre of the ritual was broken. The overpowering inevitability was robbed of its force.

The figure, once I had taken my eyes from it, somehow lost some of its influence. It stood – mute. The boys too were like death. It was as if we held an oasis of time in a frozen world.

'The end of the inscription – it reads: "*In Crispin's guise I will walk the world and my ascendancy will be complete.*" And the figure Crispin – the last figure – it is you – you turned into him and him you – you're going to be taken over.'

He pointed at the figure, but somehow something else was happening. A gathering darkness had engulfed the figure – like wings – and a sound began to fill the building like a great wind which came howling from all quarters and a fluttering as of many great wings beating the interior of the vast church through the triphorium and around the pillars. It came sweeping down upon us and the organ began to sound out of tune, a great cacophany of sound screeching higher and higher. Lamps and candlesticks tottered and crashed to the ground, a huge spiral of darkness swept the area where the figure stood, gusting the choirboys' robes. The light in the stalls flickered as if fused. The very pavement on which we stood seemed to quiver and shake, the tiles splintering under our feet.

'Hold on, Crispin. He can do nothing,' the old man shouted in my ear, holding his coat about him as if in a terrible tempest. 'He can do nothing unless you ... accept ... it's his only weakness.'

And there the figure stared, gaunt and trembling, the glowing globe held out to me. I saw the talons that held it, trembling and stretching towards me. Nearer and nearer through the screaming storm it reached, the talons stretching out towards me – a few feet – a few inches.

My uncle reached out and held my shoulders with his great warm hands, a vice-like human grasp through the storm.

'No!' I cried into the storm and the figure that was so near. '*No*! I will not accept.'

I felt myself heaved sideways by a great issue of cold air – my uncle caught me.

The globe shuddered in my sight, as if in slow motion, then the whole thing exploded inwards upon itself and with it the figure disintegrated, the robes falling to the ground – empty – and then they themselves seemingly turning to a dark liquid and running away into the cracks between the tiles of the floor.

The howling stopped – and the cacophany of sound from the organ suddenly lost its volume, wheezing and out of tune. It seemed to lose its power, as if the air that drove it was exhausted. The lights flickered and came on again.

The cathedral clock began to strike the hour. I lay in my uncle's arms, counting the strikes. *One, two, three, four, five, six.* It was six o'clock again.

*

The Bishop's reception was over – and people began to disperse – several groups walking through the chilly night down Canon's Walk. I could hear snatches of conversation from the other groups.

'Exceptional, Edwin ... a marvellous evening ... thank you ...' and from another quarter:

'How they sang ... I haven't heard anything like it since ...'

My uncle unlocked the front door, and we three made our way inside. He ushered us into the jumbled sitting room, we took our accustomed seats, and there my uncle was all ready with the brandy decanter.

He looked at me under his white bristling eyebrows – a smile playing on his lips, he poured me a large drink.

'Such a pity about the outside broadcast people having all

that trouble. I can't imagine what caused the generator failure, can you, my boy?'

I breathed in deeply. His eyes wrinkled with silent laughter and his eyebrows twitched. He was like some great benign beardless Father Christmas.

'Uncle – you amaze me.' I exhaled the breath and took the proffered glass.

He turned and gave a glass to Geoffrey, and sat down heavily into his armchair.

'And me, Canon.' Geoffrey shook his head looking at his old colleague with unconcealed admiration.

The Canon frowned into his brandy glass and spoke, as if from deep thought.

'You know, I think something will have to be done about those choristers. Did you notice how they were acting at that reception? Perfect little beasts – they had actually got a chain gang in operation putting sherry glasses under the table and out into the corridor!' He paused. 'Thank God for that ... thank God and you, dear boy ... and you.'

He leant forward and placed a large hand on my knee, shaking it gently, a deep smile of affection on his lips.

'So they've returned to normal?

It was his turn to take a deep breath.

'It would appear so. It's almost as if they had no memory of it at all. I tried to check during the evening – the occasional word or question, but they're quite as devious and naughty now as they always were. They actually thought I was on to their sherry stealing game. So it would appear that he has left them.'

'We've defeated him?' Geoffrey spoke the question from his deep armchair. The Canon didn't look up.

'It would appear so. For the time being, at least.'

It was the first chance we had had to talk since the events at six o'clock that evening.

The choristers even then had been different. They appeared almost to awake from their trance-like state, and bustle about – collecting papers and tidying. Rupert threw orders here and there, and turning to wish us good evening, as if he hadn't known we were there, and then there had been the return of the vergers and sound people, consternation over irreparable damage to the electric generator and cables; the broadcast had had to be abandoned. Then the preparations for the service itself, which was a success, the commissioned work hailed as a new masterpiece. I had even managed to sing my part – incredible that. I had only an hour before been face to face with the Abbot whose part I played in this great song of praise.

But there were many questions. I sipped my drink.

'When did you finally know, Uncle?'

'Ah ...' He held his glass with both hands. 'It fitted together when I heard about your having to take the Abbot's part in the Shepherd's Song. Remember what we had of the inscription? Well, I knew it was a prophecy. I've known that since we first began to decipher it, but I didn't know when it was to be ... actually I had thought that it was going to be Christmas – Christmas of the 700th year after Abbot Benedict began the building, but when I heard about your part in the Shepherd's Song I realised we had very little time.

'When the task is done and I am free and eighteen golden boys sing the Chant ... When the moon is full in time of high festival ... one will come of power great to take my name and state – then "in Crispin's guise".

'It was you in the Shepherd's Song taking the part ... his part, his name. The "power" was obvious too. You have great mental power – you are an outstanding academic, but you also have "the gift" – second sight, that equals 'power' in Benedict's terminology. The eighteen golden boys are plain enough – and then the rest of what we had ... "*When the moon with full rays shines from the heavens.*" It is full moon tonight – and the festival is the Septuacentenary Service. I checked – it won't be full moon at Christmas. It all made sense – but I had to know the rest. It was obvious that it was tonight but I didn't know the rest. So I managed to get out of Sister Bainbridge's hands. Not an easy thing to do, my boy, a warning for you that, never get sick during term-time. Your School Matron is a dragon ...

'Geoffrey here helped me. We managed to get away to my house, but I knew the choir were rehearsing in the cathedral – so we had time free to look at the carvings again.

'So we did. The last effigy was – or at least is as like you as a Medieval carving could be – but with the talons of something else – and the robes of an Abbot.

'The inscription took me some time to decipher. I've not your ability ... but I managed. ' *"Crispino et vutu et habitu similis per orbem terrarum pervagatus omnia sub dicionem meam redigam."* Which I read as: "Like Crispin both in appearance and dress having wandered through the lands of the world I will bring all things under my sway."

'He was going to use you, probably you and the choristers – they were to be your flock. But he needed a full-grown man with the power to shepherd them. You would have controlled them better than he did. He would only get at them because of their youth and innocence, and then only in their sleep.

'That was what you witnessed in the dormitory, and that sudden disappearance and quiet in the Song School, after their chanting – do you remember your description of them when you thought they were asleep? Their positions in their beds and the cold in the room? Their bodies were there – in the dormitory – but their spirits were elsewhere – in the Song School with him. But he needed more than their spirits. He needed them physically, and you were his vehicle. He needed to return to a physical body, to control things permanently. That was the weak link – you had to be willing.'

'But what was it that he offered me ... what was it that he held?'

He sighed.

'There are lots of descriptions. Perhaps his spirit, his psyche, the essence that has been him all these six hundred and whatever years since his mortal body was buried and decayed away. He's been about here for a very long time, and he has not been inactive ... we know that, don't we, Geoffrey?'

The elderly verger nodded.

'To our cost, I think, Canon.'

'He needed your physical frame, to dwell in you and act through you.'

'But what would have happened to me?'

'Ah – there you have it. Have another drink.' He got up and replenished our glasses, settling again to look at me. 'I suspect that what is visibly you – the Crispin we recognise – that walks and talks like you would have still been present ...' He paused looking into his glass.

'But not for long in Woolminster, I fancy. You, or your physical being, would have moved on pretty soon, I suspect – moved on to higher and more important things. You would have become a great man in education or in the Church or in the State, powerful and influential, very influential, I imagine. A force to be reckoned with, with your little flock.' He nodded in the direction of the school.

'Your disciples would have been gathered around you, but your soul ... you wouldn't have had your soul, Crispin, because it would have been him inside you, doing what he likes to do best.'

There was silence in the room. I could hear the ticking of the hall clock ... The silence extended. He drank from his glass, and stayed watching my face.

'But how could he have known all this was going to happen – the "prophecy" – all that time ago?'

He lifted a hand and pulled at his lower lip thoughtfully, his eyes wavering from my face to search the middle distance.

'What is time to him, I wonder? Those occasions we have been together, and time – what we understand of time – hasn't operated usually. Tonight – that time in your rooms – the time you told me about before. Maybe it has something to do with spirit travel, maybe anyone within the radius of his power experiences time as he does – a dual time – his and ours.'

He brought his eyes back to focus on my face.

'I don't know – I cannot tell – there are a number of things we will probably never know, like those parchment slips.' He indicated the table which the night before had held the slip of paper. The glass tumbler still stood there, but there was no parchment under it.

'It's gone, you see. What it had in it, how it worked, we won't know, nor how it went, like yours in your room. We won't know now.'

My memory clicked back – it seemed so long ago.

'The Hound – when you came to my room was that a Werewolf then?'

He smiled and settled back in his seat.

'Oh no – we haven't been dealing with werewolves, dear boy.'

His eyebrows twitched in silent laughter.

'Oh no. I think that is what you call a Familiar – hadn't it come from the carving? I think it had, you know. I believe you call it a Hound of Hell. It's quite bad enough, really. I don't think we need go into werewolves. They've never struck me as being frightfully English. Do you know what I mean?'

I could not share his mirth, but I was still puzzled.

'How did you know so much about Abbot Benedict ... and the first part of the inscription, the part about "When the task is done and I am free", what does it mean?'

'Ah ...' He looked at his old friend under his bushy eyebrows.

'Well that, Crispin, is another story.'

But Grandma, what big eyes you've got
But Grandma, what big ears you've got
But Grandma ...